FATHER WAS A
RAT KING

MANNY TORRES

UNCLE B.
PUBLICATIONS
Indianapolis, Indiana

FATHER WAS A RAT KING
An Original Uncle B. Publications Edition

Second Printing, April 2025
©2022 Manny Torres.

Photography by Manny Torres
Cover Design by Alec Cizak

ISBN: 978-1-957034-07-2

For my mother, Migna Morales
For my brothers, Carlos, Albert, Jesse and Mark
To our fathers, Angel and Wilfredo
For Humberto
For Sam

"Death is not to be parceled out as if it were a blessing."

Juan Rulfo

PART I:
There Lives a Wolf in Soledad

ONE

After the rain the city glittered like a jeweled cave. Manhattan squeezed and suffocated Soledad, leaving her exhausted. Having missed several meals this week she felt empty and transparent. But lighter meant she maneuvered faster.

Hollowness brought lucidity. The beat of her heart at her throat choked her up. She squeezed her fingers into her palms, digging her nails deeply.

Step by step slow motion of 100 frames per second. At a distance she was a blur. Hoodie pulled over her head, hiding her face. Long hair tied back and tucked behind her. She crossed a rain-slick street on a momentum of fear, driven by primal instinct. Didn't need a key, just punch open a door. Easily walk through walls. Climb into her targets. Every job was her last. Every job, young men wound up dead.

TWO

It was more an apartment than office. A startup that stalled and crashed. Small desk, a sofa and lots of boxes. Merchandise that had fallen out the back of delivery trucks. Bootlegged clothes, shoes and about seven thousand compact discs on the floor and stolen computers still in their boxes. The computer on Thiago's desk was terribly infected, the screen busy with pornographic videos that popped up and refused to go away. More of a tits and ass paperweight than anything functional.

Thiago Valoy, half-Dominican, half-Haitian, and perhaps a little Chinese sprinkled in. He looked like a fat black Buddha. Soledad sat across from him, her face stone cold with exhaustion. His computer monitor was angled in a way that allowed her to see all sorts of nastiness popping up randomly.

"You know something?" He said. "You remind me so much of Franco." He flashed a fake smile. It was the only thing separating him from other primates. With his gray suit, too much cologne and unlit cigar. Rings on every finger. On each ear.

"We share the same genes, on account he was my father," Soledad said. She was tucked inside her hooded sweatshirt like it was a wizard's cloak. She watched his hands, smelled his coffee breath.

"What's up with that black makeup and nail polish?" Thiago said.

She shrugged.

"Who you s'pose to be?"

No response.

"So what, you live in a bat cave now?" He said. "When you come for a job, you gotta consider several things. Right off the top: professionalism and presentation. This is a business I'm running here, in case you didn't notice."

"*Right*," Soledad said, scoffing at the haphazardly stacked boxes, poorly drawn graffiti posters and Black Bunny calendar from two years ago nailed to the wall. A mustache had been drawn over Miss December's upper lip, her middle teeth blackened out.

She watched his hands. The way Thiago held his toothpick was a lie. She studied the lines on his brow, the peak of his smile, the shine of his bald pate, his expressive hands. His sleepy eyes and the weight of his bottom lip; the way the toothpick rolled around his teeth. *Bogus. Forged. Phony.* There was a sick compulsion to his lying, layering one falsity over another. His disease.

She'd grown immune to it over time.

Thiago leaned to one side and pointed the toothpick at her. His "sophisticated" look.

"This is the girl I've been fooling around with." He pointed a sausage finger at a small, framed picture next to the computer monitor.

Soledad rolled her eyes. "Does your wife know?"

His brown shiny head gleamed under the overhead lamp. Layers of fat rolled just below his ears. Reminded her of a wax Buddha left out in the sun to melt.

He shook his head, rolling the toothpick end over end between his fingers. He slid it behind a rancid molar and said, "I'm living in Suffolk now, but I keep my office here. I have a neighbor I'd been watching for a while. Family man. I faked like my car got a flat in front of his house. Me and your father used to pull that shit all the time. I waited until he was taking off for work and I rolled his ass, first thing, bright and early yesterday morning, right in the middle of suburbia. Took his fucking wallet and his watch just to see if I could still jack a muthafucka. I took his shoes and told him I'd be back if he didn't send $500 to my P.O. box. Fuck him. I don't play. I'm still in the game, son. That's how your dad and me funded this organization in the early days."

"I've heard that one before."

"Yeah, yeah. I'm just letting you know I ain't done. I mean, look at me now. Look how I've expanded."

"You hit the big time all right," she said.

He looked out the window. Outside, the city was grinding.

"Baby girl don't patronize me," he said. "S'the matter witchoo? I can tell by them dark rings under your eyes you ain't sleeping well."

"Don't worry about me. I'm broke, but okay."

"You smoking weed?"

"Sometimes."

"You drinking? Taking *roxi*? *Oxy*? *X*?"

"Coffee."

"You're not eating well." Thiago nodded. "All that Chinese food ain't healthy for you."

"Not every night." She sat up and pulled back her hoodie. Her long hair was messy.

"Every morning when I get up, I drinks a glass of orange juice," he said. "I eats my carrots. You get your eyes checked lately? Too much caffeine gives you shaky hands."

She glanced at the seven empty cups of coffee gathering flies on his desk. "You've never given a shit about anybody before, certainly not me."

"You're breaking my heart." Thiago shook his toothpick at her. "I'm your godfather, baby girl. I'm here looking out for ya."

"Really? Because up to this point, I've had to handle shit by myself."

He shifted to his other side, looking concerned. "It's your stress levels. You stressing, girl. I feel you. The economy. School. Your pops dying. It's rough for a young college girl."

"I'm over it," she said.

"Don't lie."

"We weren't that close."

"I'm not gonna intrude on that," he said. "I've known you too long, baby girl."

"Don't fucking call me that."

"Yeah? Well, whatever. Do what you gotta do, booboo. Mo' money, mo' problems. Same as always. Are you sure you're all here?" He tapped his temple.

"I'm okay, if that's what you're asking," she said. "Surviving. I was up studying late."

"What you studying now?" He said. "Biology?"

"Anthropology."

"Dinosaurs and old shit? If I was you, I'd learn to cut hair or dance."

She sighed. "I'd rather deliver a few microwave ovens." Her eyes shifted towards loose merchandise laying around.

"Nah, we covered," he said. "Come summer, we'll be delivering AC units to the projects." He paused, smiling. But his eyes. Deep black eyes. "I can't believe you're the exact image of him. You look nothing like your mom. Except maybe them chink eyes."

"Heredity."

"That's what's up." From his top drawer he took out a .45 auto. It was black and greasy inside a sandwich bag. He folded his hands. Smiling. "You recognize this?"

"I don't know anything about guns," she said. "Franco used to have one."

"Show some respect. He was your dad, girl. I haven't heard you refer to him as such. *Father. Daddy.*"

"It's a habit of disassociation and disconnection."

"Oh, hello Ms. Smart Panties. Using big words and shit. You're still his little girl. He hasn't been dead that long."

"I was never a little girl."

"You don't honor him? No pictures of him on your apartment wall?"

"No. And I tore off the porno pictures he used to hang," she said. "Paint's peeling. Pipes leaking. Place is a bigger shit hole than when he was alive."

"You light candles for his birthday? ¿*Vela santa?*"

"I'm not Catholic."

"When you gonna move outta the 'jects?"

"I wish," she said. "Public housing is a fucking condo compared to that shithole on 5th. When I can afford it, I'll get out. I have school to finish."

"That's why I called you," he said.

"You got my next tuition check?"

"Smart girl." He laughed. "Smart*ass* girl. Always running your goddamn mouth."

"It hasn't been that long, *Thiggy*. I don't think we ever had the kind of camaraderie for you to talk that way to me."

"Your daddy's not here no more, baby girl." Thiago sucked his teeth. "You're all grown up now."

"I'm nineteen," she said.

"And you sure you don't remember this piece?"

"Franco's gun," she said. "So? I don't fucking want it."

"This is one *you* used."

"I just looked. I never touched them."

"What you don't know is that one day I went to see Franco," he said. "During his last days. Things had changed. For me at least. Money coming in but hemorrhaging out. And he still couldn't pull his boots up outta the shit no matter how many times me and you came to his rescue. Still doing the things I gave up doing years ago. He was desperate, just before he gave up the ghost. He felt abandoned."

Soledad crossed her arms.

"True," she said. "He wasn't around as much. Even if I was sitting next to him he was never present. He took all my shit and sold it, and just wanted to keep shooting up and smoking. Was more in love with his habit than anything else."

Thiago acted surprised. "I thought he'd cleaned up a little, started going to church."

"That didn't last. He was unbearable. Now you know."

"Now you know that I have *this*. Was all he had. He wasn't supposed to save them after a job. I had him get a new one every time, like we do. All he had to do was toss them over the George Washington after a job. Never had nothing traced back to nobody."

"He gave you that gun for drug money, didn't he?"

"I knew he was on his last breath so I got him what he wanted. I got him his last fix."

"Motherfucker…" she said.

"Show me respect, baby girl." He slapped his hands on the desk. "Imma let you slide this time. Franco said he'd had it tucked away but didn't need it no more. Maybe he kept it as a souvenir of something his little girl did. In fact, you finished it for him. You pulled the trigger."

"He talked a lot of shit," she said. "You two had that in common."

Thiago started to sweat. "But he never lied to me because he owed me his fucking life. By the way, how's your mom doing these days?"

"Running with your kind," Soledad said.

"Fuck you mean?" Thiago pushed clutter aside from the desk top. "I'm working on a new level of sophistication here. Maybe you can be in on it with us."

He leaned back and spread his arms to the glory of the room.

"I'm not using *that*." She pointed at the gun in the bag. "You want me to rob old ladies or liquor stores for petty cash? That's mad *niggerish,* bro."

"No, I'll get you a fresh piece."

"Thiago, that's not me."

"It's your fucking prints all over this piece, girl!"

"Throw it off the fucking bridge, then. *Motherfucker,* you said you had a job for me."

"Several if this works out." He dusted his sleeves. "You have a very pretty face to be talking so dirty. It excites me. I've known you since before you had tits, so looking at you that way is like looking at my own daughter."

"Franco would've killed you for talking to me this way."

"You think? You think he really cared for his family more than his habit? He was for the side that was winning. And that was all *him.* He did himself in. Someone that dead inside wouldn't give a shit." He paused and adjusted his tie. "Listen, fuck all that. It's the past. There's a reason you're here. That reason is that I need help erasing somebody. Some*bodies.* It's mad niggerish, but that's the way of the streets. When you do this, be a straight-up nigga about it. Take they wallet, steal they shit so it look like you rolled them. Even if you just throw the shit out, take it. You did enough of these with Franco to know how it's done. Blend in 'cause nobody expects a smart and pretty looking girl poppin' they ass. These ain't innocent people you taking out. They did something stupid. They owe. They fucked up and they tab is up. You not there to collect. You there to terminate accounts."

Soledad shook her head. "I don't have time for this shit. I got school."

"Course you do. I'll provide the tools. Don't be afraid to stop in occasionally. You don't even have to call. Just come right in."

"They can trace this shit."

"Not if they can't find the gun. With no witnesses it's like butter. Make sure you wear gloves. I was watching this cartoon last night and I thought of you. Some Chinese or Japanese shit. Picked the tape up on Canal St. Young girl, student. *Killer.* Turns out by day she killed and by night she was a sex robot. If you know what I mean."

"I don't think I do, Thig. If you want a sex doll why don't you buy one? You own everything else."

"Ha ha. I'm just ghetto-fabulous, baby girl. It ain't shit. Nigga-rich. Working on it, though. Stay tuned. We gonna grow this."

THREE

Days and nights passed like minutes. The sun and moon exchanged faces like time-lapsed film.

Soledad pulled the hoodie over her head and slithered like silent death down Lexington. A rambunctious preacher wailed from atop a milk crate.

"WHO YOU THINK YOU IS, BEEATCH?! I COME TO YOU IN THE NAME OF JESUS CHRIST! YOU BEST TO LISTEN, DUMB MUFUCKAS, LEST THE LORD COME AND TAKETH AWAY. AND REMEMBA, THE LORD GIVETH, THE LORD TAKETH AWAY. THE LORD GIVETH, THE LORD TAKETH AWAY..."

On the next block heading south towards Central Park a few homeboys hassled a Chinese man wearing a stained apron. They had possession of a box of fireworks and convinced him to show them how to ignite Roman candles. He lit it with his cigarette, shook and twirled it, pointing it at the sky. A shower of light erupted over her head into the street as she walked past them.

The apartment was barely a closet. It had a single bedroom, small living room space and galley kitchen. Sparsely furnished. It was empty and uncluttered. To the right was the kitchen, consisting of a small sink next to a rotting wood counter where she kept the hotplate, mini-fridge sitting on crates next to the sink. A pair of long curtains covered the doorway to the bathroom. On the opposite wall was a couch next to a cardboard set of drawers where she kept her clothes and personal items. Against the back wall was a bookshelf built from plywood and cinderblocks.

Among paperbacks and textbooks were melted candles, stacks of notebooks and toy dinosaurs.

She pinned back her curly hair and slipped into a black utility jumpsuit. Gloves, scarf and then her hooded sweatshirt. With a gun tucked in her pocket and directions in her hand, she walked back out.

A ruckus on every door stoop. The sidewalk was thick with homeboys from the neighborhood. Sometimes they'd come down from the Bronx for the fried chicken and weed.

Up to 125th in a Harlem that no longer exists. Before the condos, before white people were jogging comfortably down to the Park.

FOUR

A small woman drew Tarot cards on a table in front of the building. Opposite her was a group of men sitting on crates playing dominoes. Soledad tucked herself in her scarf and went up the stoop. They saw her but people around here minded their own business. One glimpse at the woman's table and Soledad saw the Hanged Man.

The quagmire.

Soledad waited in the lobby a few minutes until someone came down and held the door open for her. The building pulled her into its vortex of antiquity. Moldy, musty, cockroach infested. Babies crying behind thin walls, couples arguing in Spanish, cursing in English. Creaky stairways, loose banisters and dead lightbulbs. Piss puddles and a bum she could smell two floors below. When she found the apartment, she didn't have to kick open the door because it was ajar. There was only a bed and a drippy sink there. Garbage strewn everywhere. A ringed bulb buzzed from the ceiling.

The reclined man was so tall that his feet extended past the length of the bed. He wore thick glasses. His head was covered in dandruff you could see from the moon. Soledad made sure it was him, taking her all of one second to surmise, though that was never fast enough.

"I was wondering when you'd get here," the man said drawing on a cigarette. He let the ashes fall into the hair on his chest. "It was all for her. Let my history show I did it all for her. Her long hair, her beautiful makeup. The pretty green eyes. Her perfume. Is there such a thing as too much love?"

"Probably." Pointing the gun, Soledad asked if he was ready.

He closed his eyes. "I am."

"You could have just paid it all back."

"You know how quickly you burn cash on a woman who doesn't love you? You're a woman, you should know."

There was nothing dramatic in his death. A dot on the forehead, two in his heart. The gun was loud, echoing through the hallway, down to the ground floor. He died with his eyes wide open and she exited through a fire escape to the next building, over the roof and down to the opposite street.

FIVE

She followed him out of Woolworth's like any other New Yorker pressed against another, over smoky, cold sidewalks. He was wearing jeans and a Dashiki under a black leather long coat and beret. He handed some pamphlets to the Muslim brothers selling oils and incense. He grabbed a bag of potato chips at a bodega and kept moving towards 8th Ave.

"This nigga has six kids," she remembered Thiago saying. *"And two baby-mamas."*

The air smelled of sewage, roasted almonds, incense and subway lubricant. Essence of the City. She came up on him swiftly as he descended the stairs to the train depot. By the time he noticed her, he was cornered against the tile walls.

"How my kids gonna eat?" He yelled, staring up the barrel of her gun. Hands raised as if they'd deflect the bullets.

"Stand still."

She waited for the next train to enter the station with its deafening roar. The gun held 10 rounds. She shot off his fingers, pocked his forehead three times. Several rounds across his chest. Blood streaked the tiles as he went down. When he landed, she shot him two more times.

She surfaced and walked east and then cut north. Took the 4 to Bowling Green, boarded the South Ferry and casually dropped the gun in the water crossing to Staten Island. When she landed at St. George, she crossed back. Two hours later she was back home.

Overlooking the northeast corner of Central Park near Spanish Harlem, the apartment on 5th Ave. was haunted. Gathered in corners were deflated dreams, lost love and the desolate spaces of her father's memory. She could abandon it all in a blink, if it came to that. Leave it all to the bedbugs and roaches. Let it all collapse with the rest of the buildings on the block.

She placed the bag of Chinese takeaway on the kitchen table. She looked at the chair where Franco always sat, one knee up, one leg extended, his outline burned into the wall by the cathode glow of the TV. Holding a cigarette or clenching a syringe, staring directly into the TV, waiting for it to pull him into its static. Sometimes he'd turned the boom box on top of the mini-fridge full blast, his face melting in the cup of his hand.

She fell asleep on the couch without eating, waking up the next day fully dressed, feeling warm and uncomfortable. She disrobed, showered, dressed, reheated the takeaway and ate, drank coffee and walked down to Central Park.

Harlem Meer had frozen over. Seagulls slept on its iced surface. She circled the lake and walked south to the Museum of Natural History.

Lion at the impala's throat.

They have to be made an example of, Thiago had reminded her. *Breaking kneecaps and elbows don't work for me no more. When I tell you, I give these nigga's chances, I give these niggas mad breaks like I'm stupid. See, it's 'cause I spread my love too thin. And by love, I mean* my money. *Nigga's just don't wanna payback shit, nameen? Dead-ass niggas think I forget about them when I stop asking. Think they slick 'cause I known them since junior high and shit. Think I'm handing out free lunch. These jobs is coming in more frequently. Be ready.*

At the museum she stood under the giant whale for a long time, studying its mass, fascinated by the thin wires that suspended the behemoth. In the ambient darkness she moved to the insect exhibit, studying each beetle and arachnid closely. Then the gorilla and early-man exhibit. She visited every level and bought postcards at the gift shop that she later taped to the apartment walls.

Rain drizzled when she crossed Central Park West to catch a bus home. Later, the sun made a brief appearance. She ate the rest of the Chinese food by candlelight, watching the sunset in the west, behind the trees in the Park.

SIX

Blood on the tile. Not splashed or blotched. It oozed from the grout. She opened her eyes to find herself saturated, staining her hands, under her fingernails. Pouring from the old faucet. The floor covered with bloody footprints around the bathtub.

To make it go away it was necessary that she clench her eyes, close them so tight that squiggly lights appeared. Then she slowly released the tension, opening them back up to see it all fade away. The tile was mint green again, streaked only with dried soap and mildew. Half a day passed, and she was still soaking, holding her knees, shivering.

Her father, dead on the floor. Where he'd bled to death.

SEVEN

She went down for groceries. Courtyard covered in fallen leaves. Trash, broken bottles, old newspapers. An abandoned baby trolley by an overturned trashcan. Leaning against the rail of the handicap ramp was a tall skinny white guy talking to three baby-mama's. Smoking Swisher Sweets, arguing and yelling into each other's faces. She floated past them and around the corner. They barely noticed her.

At Key Food she picked up deli meats and cheese, bread, orange juice, oatmeal, produce and whatever else was on her mental list. She bought a knish and pickle as a treat. The Indian man behind the deli counter wrapped it in wax paper and smiled at her.

On the way back one of the baby-mama's blocked her access up the ramp.

"You didn't say excuse me the first time," the baby-mama said, head bobbling side-to-side.

"Don't you have a litter of piglets you should be feeding, sis?" Soledad said. The other baby-mama shoved her and the third sucker-punched her. Soledad always carried a knife but noticed that two of them were pregnant.

"Fuck off!" The white skinny guy took out a peashooter and held it sideways at her.

Soledad saw there were three little bullets in the cylinder. His knuckles were white and tight. He licked his lips nervously. She withheld her chuckle, backing down the ramp and going around to the steps into the building. She ran upstairs and peaked out of the window. It opened to 110th and the Park. She couldn't see the courtyard. To the east was the statue of Duke

Ellington and his piano. She ate sandwiches for dinner.

After considering the altercation, she dressed in her "hunting" hoodie, thought it over and then took it off. She turned on the boom box and flipped around until she found something old to listen to. She sat by the window, watching the stars come out and the way cars glittered on the street below.

Three days later, 11am and no classes. She was wondering Spanish Harlem when she saw the skinny white guy again. Open parka, flashy print t-shirt underneath. Yankees ball cap sideways and upwards. Pants hanging halfway down his legs. Big white sneakers.

She followed him to 110th instead of her usual stroll through Central Park. She went west to a bodega that was so gross she hated to go there. It always stunk of rancid meat and the ATM never worked. The white guy didn't see her creeping closely behind him as he went in to buy baby formula, lottery tickets and cigarettes.

Close enough to smell his cologne. Close enough to see the nicks where his razor had unapologetically scraped the back of his neck. Soledad let him leave the store and waited until he walked past the abandoned Dominican barbershop.

She came up behind him with knuckle-dusters and punched the back of his head. Enough to bring him down. Hat flew to the left, baby formula spilled to the right. She kicked his balls and left him moaning. By the time anyone noticed him crawling and moaning, she had flown.

EIGHT

Blood, from holes in her palms, seeping out of the lace holes of her boots, from the wound at her side. Oozing down her face from her hairline. She awoke realizing she was in The Bronx on the 1. Missed her stop by several stations. Ambulating without purpose or direction. It was all without purpose.

Oh, my fucking god, she wanted to suddenly scream to the line of commuters coming and going, walking around her. *Look at all that snow.* New York City glowed like the heart of a white sun.

Van Cortlandt Park. From there she crossed over, got on the 1 south to Harlem. Why did it take 45 minutes to go five miles? She turned her reversible coat inside-out. Walked the block several times until she saw him.

The target went up the stairwell on 125th and Broadway, constantly looking over his shoulder. She waited until he was halfway up and followed closely. Train roared overhead when she placed the 9mm at the back of his skull. His bowels gave up immediately down his legs and down the steps. Splashed her shoes like blood and brain matter splashed her arm. Leaving in haste, she forgot his wallet.

Soledad stepped over him, sprinting upstairs. She took the A going north, got off at Washington Heights, threw the gun in an open sewer line and walked across to Amsterdam. From there she took a bus to South Ferry, took a train to Brooklyn.

NINE

Spring and Summer were short. Came and went in a blur. Winter bullied itself into early December. She got off at Brooklyn Bridge-City Hall, surfacing to the stab and glare of a snowstorm that came at her unexpectedly. She'd never shot anyone in this sort of weather and was concerned with wind speeds. She'd heard about wind resistance in movies about sniper assassins but what did she really know? Did it take a physicist to explain how to kill a man? And besides, her work was always up close and personal. The snow would give her cover. Make her look like a ghost.

Sideways sleet and suddenly the bridge vanished in blinding white snow. She thought for a moment that the brick and wood bridge had broken off and drifted down the East River into the ocean. And that she was a lone human on that land ship adrift in the ocean.

She ate dim sum on Mulberry St. and wanted to watch people passing in the street from here, but other customers were breathing over her for her seat. She walked back under the columns of the municipal building. Brooklyn Bridge hadn't broken off and drifted downriver, looming closely like some brick and wood *djed*. She walked back to the train station, following her mark. 5 to the R, one train car behind, got him as he went up the stoop of his building all the way in Rego Park. Took his wallet like it was a robbery. The cash was a rare bonus. Sometimes there were food stamps.

TEN

The Number 4, Uptown. It took her three days to finally hit her next subject. He was ordinary, his face preoccupied with meeting up with Brady Keenan's wife. She had no clue who that was, but that was the name Thiago had mentioned when he gave her the job.

The train ran late.

Sometimes Soledad would catch this man smiling to himself as she lingered closely. He looked back and all he could see was the bottom of her face from under the hood. He waited close to the platform edge, ready to bum rush into the car as the Bronx Express sliced into the station. The crowd surged forward. She let go the gun in her pocket and got up on him, pushing him into the face of the train.

It happened faster than she'd anticipated. The impact tore him in half. He went crashing against the safety gate at the end of the platform, splattering several passengers with viscera. She slipped backwards toward the exit as the crowd huddled over his body parts. When she surfaced, she ran, holding the gun deep in her pocket.

ELEVEN

Soledad always knew what she would do if she was on her own. While standing over the grave the military gave her father, she felt sad but couldn't cry. The churchman said some words, the rifles saluted. They lowered the casket into the narrow grave. A single white slab remained in his honor.

Franco's cousin and her mother had been there. At first, she hadn't recognized the skinny, tacky woman wearing big sunglasses on that cloudy gray day. Dressed like some neon harlequin in a teal skirt, yellow shirt and red clogs.

"You're working in the city now?" her mother asked.

"Mostly school," Soledad said. At times her mother looked younger than she did, a tiny, pale occidental in bright clothes.

"Did you get the sneakers I sent you for Christmas?" her mother said.

"Yeah. I'll wear them in the summer."

"'Cause I didn't get a thank you card."

"There was no return address."

"Hmm."

They walked toward the black service van that had driven them out to Long Island for the service. Franco's cousin sat quietly in the back. They were strangers.

"I still have your photo albums," Soledad said. "Pictures of your family. People I've never met."

"Your father never met them either," her mother said.

"When was the last time you saw your family?

"They don't even know I exist."

"Hmm."

"The albums are boxed up, one on top of the other in a damp corner in my dresser."

Her mother shrugged. "You can keep them. Did Franco leave you anything?"

"I've been emancipated for some time now. I get to collect his social security pension as long as I'm in school."

"That's great." The little woman touched her daughter's face. Soledad attempted to draw something from it, but the touch was cold. "You coming back to Florida?"

"Most likely, not." Soledad said. "There's nothing for me down there. I'd just get in your way from whatever it is that you do."

They parted with her mom making false promises.

Back at the apartment, Soledad stared into a faded photo of her mother and father looking happy with a younger her in between them. Through osmosis or Stendhal phenomena she melted into the photo, and she was there with them now, for that moment immortalized between them.

TWELVE

Two blocks from the apartment and it began to rain. Cold, hard, winter rain. She ducked into the cathedral on the corner of Malcolm X and 110th. The cathedral was a warehouse. Observing the service in session, she concluded that all devotees of all doctrines were lunatics. *Fucking nuts.* Screaming or crying about it wouldn't have helped so instead she listened to a woman preaching to a group of youths in Spanish. Not understanding much of it but grateful for the temporary shelter.

Soledad closed her eyes, but not to pray. She could have easily slept right there in the warm comfort of the temple.

"There's no god what created us."

She turned her head, superstitious about looking over her shoulder and finding the devil staring back.

And there he was.

"It's this idea of a greater father," the man said. "Something we, as cells, reach for. Look at all their faces. They look lost to you? Do you ever wonder what their sins were? The worst, I imagine. What are yours?"

"I-" She was upset that she hadn't noticed him until he was within arm's reach, one pew back.

"You're just waiting out the rain, I know," he said. "I haven't seen you here before."

"I won't be long," she said. "I won't interrupt your service."

"It isn't mine to disrupt."

Soledad stood up and walked out. Very wet and cold outside. The street sizzled with rain and passing cars. The trees in Central Park looked like gnarled, old hands. The park looked haunted. She took the long walk home for safety reasons.

The tall man followed in the hazy light. Close to 6'5", skinny but not clumsy. Of prehistoric sophistication. He'd been around for millennia but he in no way looked old. His primitive pale face contrasted his dark suit, his raven hair neatly slicked back. Whether he was there or a cipher was not clear, but he was following her, that was certain.

"You're all over the place these days," he said. He paced several feet behind her.

She walked as far ahead as she could, but he caught up, walking beside her. "You following me?"

"Observing you," he said. "You know this neighborhood. I'd like to put you to work."

"I don't work for pimps."

"I don't peddle flesh. But I do provide all sorts of services to people who pay a lot."

Soledad circled the opposite direction. "I'm not a fucking mule."

"You've done some work for Thiago," he said.

"It's not the first time we've met."

"Who?" she said.

"Your father's friend."

Soledad walked straight instead of turning the corner, not looking back at him.

"Who the fuck are you?" she said.

"I've disassociated with all identity baggage," he said. "But, as a formality, call me Leo Kern. You don't have to say yes to anything I'm offering right now. Here's my card." He reached over her shoulder and she snatched it. Took one look at it and flung it into the wet street.

"No matter," he said. "I'll probably see you around. Go to church much?"

"Not really." She crossed another street, moving further away from the direction of her apartment.

"Be careful," he said watching her walk off. "Been a lot of shootings around here lately."

THIRTEEN

Registration day. Someone had scribbled *Check gas, long bridge ahead…* on a community board that had not seen this much abuse in a single day. Six hours and just now she was coming up on the window.

Soledad reached it, slipped her schedule through the slot. A pretty coed with glasses looked it over. Checked her computer. Twisted her mouth, confused but said nothing. She mentioned something to the girl behind her before giving Soledad an exuberant quote for her classes.

"That's covered by the loan," Soledad said.

"No, it's not," the girl with the glasses said.

"It was approved. They covered my last semester."

"You see that?" The girl showed her some numbers on her screen. The bottom three were in the negative. "Go talk to the financial aid counselor, then come back."

Soledad rolled her eyes and moved to a waiting area where thirty other losers like her stood around looking sleepy and hungry. When her number was called her blood sugar was low and she wasn't really listening.

"Your social security benefits ended." They told her. "You're 18 now."

"And that's exactly why I should qualify for *this*." Soledad pressed her document so hard she almost poked a hole in it.

"You can look through the catalogue but it's not going to cover you until next semester."

"You know, I'm six credits short. *Six*."

"I know, dear. You didn't qualify for this one because of your grades."

"Well, I thought the loan would cover two semesters."

"You probably didn't calculate your books, huh?"

"Probably not. I can always transfer."

"You can't until payments are made. Or other payment arrangements made."

FOURTEEN

Ancient and decrepit remains of the Algonquian and Dutch exchange. Gothic castles of a slowly collapsing kingdom. Overcrowded with every ethnicity and culture in the entire world. New York City was a rabbit hole to descend or get sucked into, depending whom you asked. A vortex, some would say, mostly those who wanted to get out.

On the train a man sat across from her reading The NY Times. He'd folded it open to page six. At the bottom of the page she saw a write-up about a shooting of a random pedestrian. Something about shootings in the area and she knew Thiago would mention it to her next time she saw him. He did read the papers. Mostly for sports.

The violence was blamed on gang activity in the area north of 125th St. They said this kind of thing was going away now that cops were stopping and frisking more and new construction was going up in crime ridden neighborhoods.

Soledad read as much of the article as she could and then turned to search the map behind her, following the red dot marking each station, counting off the stops until she reached home.

FIFTEEN

Rain, distant sirens. Ambulance lights against brick and glass textures of the city. And then silence. No shadows, only chiaroscuro. The world may as well have been dead, humanity extinct for what was a Sunday night in the city.

"No one will ever believe a girl could do all this. No one would ever suspect *me*," is what Soledad told Thiago at his office.

He was wheezing with anger. "You think I'm too stupid to know, but I know. I read the papers too."

Eating chicken wings his driver/assistant had picked up from a pizza and waffle joint on Malcolm X.

"You sloppy." He swigged down old coffee from a blue Styrofoam cup. His lips snapped and popped. "You leaving bodies everywhere."

"You think I'm supposed to carry a trash bag with me to clean up?" Soledad said. "Send somebody else to clean it. They die where I leave them."

"That's not the point. You in the papers, girl!"

"Not me. There's no description of a suspect. They called it 'gang related'. There were three in one month. What the fuck you expect?"

"Relax," he said.

"You fucking relax."

"I'm saying, you can't just leave them laying around. You been leaving they wallets too. You s'pose to be robbin' them."

"They always shit their pants," she said.

"Well, you wearin' gloves, ain't you? You can't just leave them like that."

"Stop paying me to kill people."

"Girl!" Thiago pounded his desk. When his tantrum was over he finished eating, licking his fingers in a way that turned her stomach. He put his hands together as if in prayer. He exhaled.

"Listen," he said. "Forget all this for now. Let's talk about *you* for a minute. Do you have love in your life?"

"What? I thought you were going to ask me if I had 'god' in my life."

"Well, god is love. To find it you have to have the other."

"That makes no sense," she said. "I don't have either."

"Listen…"

"Like, do I have a boyfriend?" she said.

"Is there love left in you? I mean, you need it to stay alive. I have it in my life."

"You mean those chickenhead, project hoe's you roll with?"

Thiago pounded his fists again and she tilted her head until her neck crackled. She broke a little smile. He straightened his tie. Grease and sauce had stenciled around it against his shirt.

"What's gonna happen to your soul?" he asked. "You can't do this for always. I mean, you're going to go crazy if you think you can hold out."

"You sound like you're trying to talk me out of it," she said. "Does this mean our deal is off? Or are you stifling your guilt? Because I know how you run shit."

"I felt angry and I told you off," he said. "I just want an answer. What's in you?"

Soledad looked away. *"Nothing."*

He chuckled. "You're cold and distant. Just like a woman."

"You want me to show remorse for what I do? If I did, I wouldn't be doing it."

"Girl, I know you scared," he said.

"Not scared of you." She leaned forward. "Everything that you're about, and everything you're going to say, I already know, so keep it to yourself. *You are not a good person.* But you seem to know best, huh *ghetto-godfather?* You're the one forced me into this business. Why would a girl complain when she's being taken care of? When something else more exciting comes along, let me know. I'd like to jump on that bandwagon. You wanna know something else? I don't look at their faces when I shoot them."

SIXTEEN

Her memory of most people was their trifling presence and banal conversation. She was on the train and from the moment she heard, *"Is Coltrane even relevant anymore?"* she knew what she was in for. A tubby bald guy who was 26 but looked 39. Graduate students in a cluster. Lipstick anarchists. *Tankies.* Some hippie clown sitting on the floor of the train car with his back against the pole. Nobody, but nobody should ever sit on a subway car floor. Any New Yorker will tell you. Even the dirtiest, filthiest hobo didn't sit on the subway floor. This guy did. The group looked like they were heading to some Brooklyn dungeon to talk about Charlie Kaufman movies.

Three broke off from the group and she followed them. Soledad pulled her hoodie up over her head and robbed them at gunpoint, making them get on their knees on the station platform.

When she woke up the next day at the apartment on 5th Ave. she couldn't remember where all those extra phones had come from. She took them down the hall and dumped them down the incinerator. Thiago had a merchandise guy but the thought of hawking this shit off to him made her want to burn it all.

SEVENTEEN

Union Square station under reconstruction. Getting to her platform meant rushing around a low-lit, plywood maze. In a city of 11,000,000 she was suddenly alone in this desolate, subterranean passageway. She sat in an empty corner of the train car. Seven stations before her stop she smelled smoke.

She closed her eyes and leaned back. She'd learned to sleep on the train but had to focus on not missing her stop. Or fall into a deep sleep and wind up in The Bronx.

"Sir. Excuse me, sir."

Soledad turned her head to see the woman who spoke. Wearing a leopard print coat and hat, the woman held a copy of the New York Post. On the cover was a photograph of a wolf with glowing eyes. He'd been found loose in Central Park last night. Last of his kind.

"Sir, this is a no-smoking train. *Hello?* Sir." Her corrosive accent was a vanishing vernacular. *"This is a no-smoking train, do you hear me?"*

The man in the beige coat and floppy hat sat there smoking discreetly, doing the crossword.

The lady looked around. The train was empty except for them. "Do you believe this?" She asked Soledad. "That's why people die of cancer every day. Oh my gawd! You're choking up the train, sir. *Sir.* You're gonna get a ticket. Sir, you're gonna get a ticket. Do you want me to find the conductor? *Where's the MTA cops?"*

Soledad stiffened. Her station felt a million miles away. The train slowed, rattling and squeaking as it curved and slithered through the bowels of the city.

Soledad saw the woman reach up and snatch the cigarette from the man's face.

The man, suddenly awake with rage, shoved her back and stabbed her breasts and throat with his pencil. The woman wailed, vomiting blood.

"Stop it! Help! Help!" she screamed.

She stumbled over on Soledad's lap, smearing her with blood. Next station was announced. Soledad pushed her off and the man came for both of them, holding his bloody pencil like a knife.

She shot the man through the hoodie pocket, thru the center of his forehead. The lady's face contorted with terror. The bottom of her face was a cascade of cruor.

With cold animal instinct, Soledad shot her face. The train lurched into the station and slowly halted. Soledad took off quickly, threw herself down some stairs, twisting her ankle. She limped most of the way home, wondering how long her weak ankle would hold. Wondering how she would tell Thiago that she failed again.

EIGHTEEN

"**S**hooting people on the train? You tryin' to invoke my rage? Is that what you're doing now?" Thiago choked on a greasy piece of chicken. "You know what somebody told me yesterday? '*He who laughs last casts the first stone.*' You know what that means? It means your first action leads to a whole lotta trouble after."

"He just kept stabbing her." Soledad recalled, her complexion turning avocado. Her bottom lip quivered. Not with nervousness but nausea.

He'd learned to listen to her low, barely audible tone.

"The TV news said the lady got shot," Thiago said. "*Are you fucking crazy?* That's what I'm asking. Are you fucking crazy? And also, *what the fuck is the matter with you?*"

"That lady was fucking crazy," she said. "She provoked that man. You could just see her crazy. Her face was all red and she was on the brink."

"Little girl," Thiago said. "I've seen them too. But I don't get the urge to kill them. You can see it in their lit faces everywhere you go. Glowing neon pink. You know what makes white people do that? Prescription drugs. I seen the ads on the bus and shit. For bipolar shit. Stress. Depression. People who can't sleep. Pill poppers. *Gump gump gump.* Uppers, downers. *Sideways.* And now, people are just exploding. Gonna get crazy bad after a while."

"I had to defend myself!" she said. The man turned on me.

She was just an accident. She was going to bleed to death anyway."

Thiago squeezed the napkin in his hands until it bled orange hot sauce. "Franco would have fucking killed you for something this stupid. And if your pops had ever done shit like that...I..."

"Franco loved me, and he wouldn't have done shit to me. You would have killed him. Just say it." Soledad wished she could chunder across his desk, colorful Chinese delivery upchucked over his lunch basket. "Say it. Be transparent, you bastard. You're supposed to have my back, chump."

He wiped his mouth. "You know what? You fucked up. I have to keep things really low now. That's going to cost me, so Imma cut you off. You didn't do the job and caused too much exposure. In the meantime, you're suspended indefinitely."

"We've—I've never fucked anything up. I've done everything you asked."

"Get out of my fucking face," he said. "You're suspended."

Soledad chortled through her nose. So close. Puke was at her throat but wouldn't rise to her mouth.

"Fucking bitch," Thiago said. "Watch your back is all Imma say."

"Why not kill me now? Save yourself the cash you're going to pay some crackhead to do it."

"Get the fuck out. Go."

NINETEEN

Soledad walked, hands tucked in her hoodie pockets. Holding the gun for comfort. Leo Kern intercepted, having walked away from a guy on a wheelchair he'd been speaking to. The guy rolled off and caught a bus on 5th and 96th.

"That guy I was talking to," Kern said. "Ex-military. Dishonorably discharged for blowing up a supply room. That's how he got the plastic legs and plastic shit bag hooked to his waistband. I give him work when I can."

Walking steady, not looking at him, she said,

"What kind of work?"

"Not too different from what you do," Kern said.

"I'm a student, man. I don't know what you think it is I do. Looks like you're exploiting the handicap."

"I provide work. He's out on 125th every day, rattling his cup full of change. I can always use his skillset."

"You don't talk like a mob man," she said.

"I'm not. *We're* a little more advanced."

"*We?*"

They stopped at the corner. He was very much the tall, slender boogieman looking down at her.

"When you're ready to work for me, let me know." He crossed, looking back at her. "Make a change in your life. *Permanent change.* Unless you just want to sit around and let this city consume you."

**Part II: Soul Dad
(Baltimore and New York)**

ONE

If she'd seen one deserted train station in a city of blight, she'd seen them all. The smell, steam and pollution alerted her to what kind of place she was going to and the type of people that lived there.

Sixteen, traveling northward with money her mother had given her before leaving for Miami. The farewell was brief, Soledad unable to imagine coming out of this little Japanese woman's loins.

"Was I switched at birth?" she asked, to which her mother only giggled a response. "Just because I'm old enough doesn't mean I really want to go there."

"Come on, baby." Her mother pinched her cheek. "You don't miss daddy? It's been years since you seen him. You old enough to go now. He'll be happy seen you."

"He'd be happy to see you too."

"Oh no," her mother had said. "You know that can't happen. He happy to see you now. He need you."

"But I can't care for him. He's a grown man. It's really not fair."

"You tell him that when you see him. You tell the man who fought so hard for America and then sent you money every Christmas that you won't see him."

The station echoed like a cave when she'd said that. Her mother's words played over and over in Soledad's head for a long time.

"Have to go work in Miami. You'll be okay." Her mother had said, walking away, waving goodbye.

Soledad knew she'd see her again, but not too soon. The station had been empty, but she found an echoing comfort in the loneliness. She'd boarded and spent the next thirteen hours reading and sleeping on the train.

Rain drops against the window as the train sped into Baltimore. Epic, lucid dreams exhausted her. She awoke just as the train arrived. Down the stairs, past a drunken Santa Claus collecting change for the rescue mission, singing one verse of "This Old Man" over and over with perverse glee,

"This old man, he played six, he played knick-knock on their dicks…"

Soledad walked from the station straight to the VA hospital, a ragged edifice filled with old furniture and hollow men.

Franco was half the man she remembered. Right arm in a sling, bandages and gauze wrapped around his head.

"I had a dream that you came to see me." Franco told her from the hospital bed, arms IV'd. He wasn't at all surprised when she'd entered the room. "C'mere and gimme a kiss, girl. Didn't you miss your old man?"

Soledad looked neither happy nor sad, feeling pity for this frail man who'd once carried her mother and her in each arm around their house in Central Florida.

"Mom said you tried to kill yourself." She said in his ear as he smothered her with kisses. Beard bristle reddened her cheek.

Franco laughed. He was hoarse and gravelly. He had a slight Puerto Rican accent. "I know I told you this before: your mother's fucking crazy. She sent you here 'cause she's irresponsible and can't even take care of *herself.*"

"She said the same thing about you."

"So, what? You got kicked out of school? Whatcha doing here? Been misbehaving?"

"If I got in trouble, I'd have nobody to bail me out, so no, I'm not in any trouble."

"Bah. You getting into it with boys?"

"Not really," she said. "I graduated early."

"And you spending vacation with your daddy? That's sweet."

"I wanted to make sure you were... still alive."

Franco started sobbing. "Appreciate you coming up to take care of me, baby."

Her hand snaked toward his, clenching his rough fingers. Avoiding the bandage covering the IV needle. "I didn't say I'd take care of you. I'll stick around until you're better, then I'm going back."

"Where the hell you gonna go to? Ain't your mom move away?"

"She said she found work in Miami. I'm going to start taking early classes and try to get into a university. We'll see where I wind up." Her eyes pulled away from him to the machines, dials and digital displays. "Why did you hurt yourself?"

He cleared his throat. "You're not going to believe this."

"Convince me." Soledad pulled up the guest seat and sat.

"Listen," Franco said. "I was out of bus fare. You gotta believe me."

It was then she noticed the scabs and dry holes at the pits of his elbows. Other older marks ran up his arms. Little pink skin dots against his light brown skin.

"A friend of mine drives a garbage truck so I hopped on for a few blocks," Franco said. "Needed to get my VA check cashed. He took the turn too hard and fast, and I landed on my face. Broke my wrist. Busted up my face. Well, it's an improvement, right?"

"When are they going to let you out?"

"With supervision, I can leave tomorrow," he said. "They have to supervise my sleep, make sure I don't slip into a coma. They'll give me a sermon and some painkillers."

She'd slept in the hospital that night. The next afternoon she paid their cab fare back to his walkup on Lombard St. in Butcher's Hill. Where the sidewalks were more dog shit than concrete. A church on every corner with an Irish pub next door.

Soledad arrived with only a small bag and suitcase. He helped carry the suitcase, smiling even though there was a look of unease and dissatisfaction on her face. The apartment was a shamble. Old furniture. Beer bottles everywhere. Rags for clothes, dirty disposable plates everywhere, lampshades laminated with pages from Hustler. Explicit nudes pasted on the walls.

When she'd settled in, they sat at an old wobbly poker table, a dim bulb above their heads. They sat frozen like an old moody painting. He'd swept all the old empty bean and vegetable cans off to make space for dinner. They ate canned ravioli cooked on a hotplate. Washed it down with soda. The small TV buzzed beside them.

"Don't you have any fruit?" Soledad said.

"Nah," Franco said. He sounded tired and raspy like an old blues singer. "Sometimes I buy some from the Mexicans, but it always rots."

"You're supposed to eat it, not let it go bad." Franco agreed.

"How'd you get here?" he said.

"Took a train."

"By yourself?"

Soledad nodded. "I know it's been a while, but you know, I can take care of myself. I do a lot of things by myself."

"You know my house is open for you, baby." Franco said. "*Para siempre.*" He reached over and with his good hand, held hers. "I get food stamps and a small check on the first and fifteenth. It's not a lot, though. I don't have a computer or video games or cable TV. And this neighborhood is fucking busted, so I don't expect you to go outside." He sniffed and shoveled food in his mouth, chewing and snapping his lips.

"That's okay," she said. "I read a lot. I can at least go to the library." She paused, pushed the ravioli around the plate. "Your bathroom is dirty."

"I'll clean it," Franco said. "How long you staying?"

"Probably until fall."

"Where you staying when you go back?"

"I know some people," she said. "Why does it even matter? I've been taking care of myself. I'll manage."

He finished eating and crossed his arms. "That breaks my heart when you say that."

"Try to see it from my viewpoint, *Franco.* If you can."

"C'mon, girl. You can call me dad."

"I know," Soledad said. "Things were pretty fucked up before you left and moved here. Mom said you were sick, but you didn't want to get help. I was young but I remember that shit. You were always out of it. Sleeping all the time. Cracked out or something."

Frank looked regretful.

"I got this job at a warehouse," he said. "We pack porno magazines to be shipped overseas. You believe that?"

Soledad nodded. "Well, stick with that. Okay? It's work. I'll help change your bandages."

Franco smiled.

"Okay," he said. "The VA ain't gonna do shit for me anyway. They couldn't fix my head. They gave me a script, but it might as well be baby aspirin. *Shit don't work.* They said I have to go talk to a counselor once a week. Why? I don't have time for that shit. They make me say things that make me mad or make me sad. Fuck that shit."

She rolled her eyes. "Yeah, I can see there's no time in your busy schedule. And how do you afford all this junk food?"

He laughed and shook his head in denial. Only to her. "The Mexican store gives me credit."

Then he pleaded, "Baby, please believe me. I needed a ride to the VA. That's how I got hurt. I didn't even have change for the bus. At least I'm still alive." He chuckled. "They couldn't kill me in the desert, they can't kill me here."

"But that war… was a long time ago," Soledad said. "You haven't gotten the kind of help you need. Help to get your head straight. You have to go to those meetings, even if you hate them. You can't just dabble in it."

"Listen to you," Franco said. "You suddenly father to the man. Truth is, nothing really fixes it. You either die *over there* or die slowly when you get back home. There's no cure. But I promise you, I'm fine. Patriots wave their flags and plaster 'support our troops' stickers all over they ass, but when muthafuckas come home we get a lot of doors slammed in our faces."

"You're feeling like you're still over there," she said. "Even after all this time."

"Relapses, honey. You can't get over some of that shit. You carry it forever. How's your mother looking?"

"Beautiful, I guess."

"I used to write her poems."

Soledad rolled her eyes. "I remember once when she wasn't looking you wrote her a note on a napkin."

"She probably threw all that shit out after I left."

"No, I saw her blow her nose with it when you went to get more beer." They laughed.

TWO

Franco showed her the neighborhood. He escorted her down its many blighted streets, introduced her to every bum, prostitute, transient, and crackhead he was acquainted with. They passed some hobos warming over a flaming steel drum, singing. They banged pipes against the drum sides, dancing and having a good time at it. They waved as they passed.

'*My people*', Franco called them. There wasn't a single corner depleted of some criminal element. Everyone on the street knew Franco Castillo. Crack-slinging homeboys, even the cops. Tall, cross-dressed, or trans-prostitutes winked and waved. Franco smiled and waved back.

"More sordid than Florida," Soledad said.

"More what?"

"It stinks."

"That smell? It's the power plant," Franco said. "These are 'my people'. *Mi gente. Son mis amigos.*"

"People are people. Anywhere you go a ghetto is a ghetto."

"Don't say that too loud. What did you say you were studying? That book you were reading. The one about social-economic stuff?"

"*A Short History of Decay.* Cioran," she said. "Yeah. That's this, right here. Why do poor people have to live like this? Would it kill them to bend over and pick up some of this trash?"

Franco laughed.

"Probably," he said. "*You're* poor people now. Just like me. But one day I'll buy you a condo in Florida."

"How about paying for my school first?"

"Can't be that bad down there," Franco said. "You got beaches and sunny weather."

"If it had been anywhere else, I would have stayed. Everybody speaks Spanish. I don't speak Spanish, but they think I do because of my name."

"What's wrong with speaking Spanish? I speak Spanish. How come you didn't learn?"

"Mom said you didn't want me speaking Spanish."

"Get the hell out of here," Franco said. "When did I say that?"

"I wouldn't know. I was too young to remember. Probably because you didn't want people discriminating against me."

"Probably," he said. "I said a lot of stupid shit back then. You date anybody? Boyfriend?"

"Not really," she said. "It's a waste of time. I don't think I'm going back."

"Well, you're here now. You got me, I got you. We're all we got."

She paused. "I wanted you to know that I'm not mad at you and I don't hate you, dad. I know Mom abandoned you. There's no denying that."

"I abandoned *myself*," he said "It wasn't just being away. Sometimes vice meant more than family."

"You got a long way to go to get over your vice."

"It's this environment. The people that come in and out of my life. People trap you in their situations. They come to you all friendly but infect you with their *vice*. The fact that your mother wouldn't come but sent you shows you what a fucking coward she is."

"Would you rather I wasn't here?"

"No, sweetie. I'm blessed having you here. My kingdom is yours. Sorry that I don't have more to give you."

She said, "All we ever really own is our death, Franco. You got a good grip on that. You're the ruler in this rat kingdom."

He put his arm around her shoulder and brought her close to his chest.

"I don't know that I'm capable of ruling shit," he said. "Don't be so goddamn cynical. It's all those philosophical books they got you reading."

"Yes, they force me to read all these anti-establishment tomes." She shook her head.

"Well, your mother slept with her bible. She ever force you to go to church?"

"A few times. Until I cursed out the Sunday school teacher."

Franco laughed.

"Mom got tired of yelling at me and being embarrassed about it," Soledad said. "So she just let me do what I wanted."

"Compared to her, you think maybe I'm more optimistic?" Franco said.

"Delusional, maybe," she said. "Mom is fatalistic. It's her Asian blood. I have an image she painted of you. Not like on canvas or paper. In my head. It took me several years to erase it."

"Your mom, well, your mom is *oblivious*," Franco said.

"Maybe we all are," she said. "She's missing something. And it makes her sad. But she doesn't show it or mention it to me, ever. I've understood my place in the world. It's a shit place."

"God has a way of showing his sadness."

"Is that what it is? He's crying the river of the world's misery and we're drinking it. If he really existed, he seems like he'd be more pissed than sad."

"You gotta give Him a chance," he said.

"Is that who you're waiting on? 'Cause you look a little neglected. Like you got left at the station, and your god passed you by."

"Deflated," Franco said. "A little fucked up."

"A little?"

"I say my prayers."

"I stopped praying a long time ago," she said. "It happened the time I asked, *'why have you forsaken me?'* and god answered, *'because I don't exist'.*"

"What about your soul?"

"I'm sure whatever is there will have to exit somewhere when I'm done," she said.

"You gotta believe that there's something bigger."

"Suddenly you're born again?"

"It's something that keeps me going, Praise the Lord. We die every day but why do we wake up every day and do it over?"

"Sounds like half-ass optimism," Soledad said. "Sounds like desperation. You sound hopefully unconvincing. The thought process of praising a god doesn't explain violence or war. I don't believe in heaven."

"Baby girl, where you gonna go when you die?"

"Some days I feel like I'm between here and there, to be honest. The idea of god discredits man and everything he's achieved."

"But without god, man would not have pushed forward in this miserable fucking world," Franco said.

"Jesus only loves a man who loses. Look, I'm not negotiating anything. I can't take away that thing that brings your comfort. I'm not going to quash your faith."

"You're too young to have given it that much thought, girl."

"Don't condescend my age, *old man*. I know why people believe what they believe. Life is misery, unpleasantness and suffering."

"*Lots of suffering.*"

"God is a concept to make sense of it all."

"But you've never read a bible."

"I didn't say that," she said. "Mom has one. It's the greatest compilation of lunatics ever written. Pillars of salt, murdered babies; all that shit. Everybody has to find a go-to thing for relief. You think that fix will ever replace your current one?"

Frank had no answer.

THREE

They would sometimes play checkers on the kitchen table. Or she would read while he watched old horror movies on TV. The old creaky sofa was her bed. Sometimes he'd be on the bathroom floor shivering. Swearing he hadn't taken anything all week, could she spare a couple of bucks. He quit narcotics but drank with a vengeance. He'd stand in the dark bathroom stiff but poisoned by the fifth of vodka he'd down in one gulp. Eyes wide and scared.

Her mother wasn't accepting her collect calls anymore.

Soledad spent the next month making paltry meals for them both, watching the little black and white TV he kept on a milk crate. It tended to overheat and shut off, usually in the middle of an action scene from *Starsky & Hutch*.

Franco had a way of rehabilitating, not only healing but *resurrecting*. He gained some weight in that time she was cooking for them and back to not being around much. Like when she was a child. She would clean and buy groceries with her dwindling savings. Most afternoons were spent studying at Enoch Pratt Library.

Soledad hated being out past six, but certainly the city hated her more. Daylight vanished around 5:30 every day in the fall. She came home to the lights being shut off, but several candles taken from the dumpster of the Catholic church up the block lit up the apartment.

Franco limped around out of his mind. The apartment smelled like he'd been sniffing chemicals, but she didn't mention it.

"You still remember me teaching you how to box?" He said from his mattress on the floor. "You broke my nose. My little girl broke my fucking nose."

Soledad put away the groceries in the small cabinet covered in roach shit and sat across him on the mattress. Franco procured a gun from under his pillow, dismantling it.

"I wanted to name you Diva Nicole, but I think I slurred my words," he said. "Your mother said I was too drunk so she said I should name you after your grandmother, my mother."

"You told me that story before."

They were half-circled by bright candles.

"You see this?" He nodded, polishing the .45 auto, possibly the newest, shiniest thing in the apartment. He placed the weapon parts between them. "This is yours. In a few years, when you're old enough, this will be yours to keep. Right now, it's my moneymaker. Bread winner. Some men, they steal bread for their family. I'm not one of those."

Her eyes, glossy and wide, expressed two things: malevolence and fear.

"I don't want no bread," he said. "*Yo quiero mi* caviar. I gotta do this thing now. My list piled up. I've fallen a little behind. Did some favors, now I'm in deep. There's only so many things a vet can do once the war is over, right? So, I went and did what I know how to do."

"You're robbing liquor stores?"

"That's low-class, baby. It's just… this one last time and then I'm out."

"You said your list piled up."

"Here, put this gun back together. Need more lighting."

She walked to the dresser and lit another candle. Sitting in a lotus position she began to reassemble the gun under his slow, slurred instructions. Took her several tries to lessen her assembly time, but she quickly learned.

"If I don't do this I won't get out," Franco said. "I feel like I'll never get out."

"You can always move away."

"I'll never get out of here."

"You can go back home to New York," she said.

"You think your mother might move up here?"

"Doubt it. At least you're not kicking me out like she did."

"You want to stay here forever?" He said.

"For *never.*"

"You and me both. I need to go down to Canton Park and do this thing."

"You can barely move from here to the bathroom."

"Fuck it, then." He grabbed the gun, stood up and then tucked it behind his pants. "Imma limp down to the bus stop." He laughed.

"Your stitches haven't come out yet. Your wrist is still busted."

"The other hand works just fine. This job is easy. Just one man. That's how you do it. One man at a time."

FOUR

Two months in Baltimore was an eternity in hell.

She was wearing jeans and a coat, her Converse sneakers without socks. On the way up the Hill two girls aggressively approached. They shoved her against a safety fence surrounding a burned-out walkup. Soledad skidded and landed on her butt. One of the girls kicked her books into the street. They came at her, grabbing her hair and yanking until tears welled up. They stepped off and gave her a chance to stand up. Soledad readied her fist when Franco showed up and pulled both girls back. He grabbed them by the neck and yanked them to the ground. He slapped them hard across their faces, yelling,

"*Next time you touch her, I'll kill you, your mother, AND your father! You hear me you, little black bitches?!*"

"*My daddy's in jail!*" One of them yelled tearfully.

He clawed their throats. "Goddamn it, I will commit a fucking crime, get arrested and kill him in jail! *You hear me?*"

He shook them and released, watching them run downhill, palms against their bruised faces. Franco grabbed Soledad by the arm and rushed her home. The fastest five blocks she'd ever walked. Upstairs he sat her down in the kitchen and paced. Violence had woken him from his daily petrification. It was the soberest she'd seen him.

"Listen baby," he said. "I should have told you. If someone is brave enough to knock you down, you better get up and make them regret they laid hands on you. Little boys and even little bitches like those. What happened to the boxing moves I showed you?"

"I didn't see them coming."

"I know what we're going to have to do."

"Get me the fuck out of Baltimore?"

"Can you not talk like that?"

"Sorry."

"Don't trust nobody," he said. "Fuck 'em. If they think they're so big and bad, then they're big and bad enough to take a punch. Kick their faces. Kick their fucking teeth in. You come from strong blood, *hija.* Don't take no shit." He stopped, craned his head at the window. "Stay here. Don't open the door until I come back."

Franco ran downstairs and crossed the street. Soledad tracked him down the Hill as he confronted a man who started yelling in his face. One of the two girls who'd attacked her was there beside him. He was a rotund man with shiny uncombed hair. Franco proceeded to wreck his face, punch after punch while his daughter watched and cried for him to stop. The man slid on a dog shit landmine and fell on his ass. He lay bleeding while Franco screamed at his daughter. Franco looked up at Soledad watching from the third story window and froze. He pushed the girl away and walked down Lombard. Soledad didn't see him for two days.

FIVE

Soledad had watched the world plenty from that window, knowing this wasn't the whole world. Often times she watched Franco from up there, in the street shaking hands with shady types.

In the morning, she found him sleeping on his mattress. Less bandages as the wounds healed. His arms looked dry. Downstairs a car honked. People called his name.

Soledad stumbled off the sofa to wake him, but he wouldn't wake up. He turned over and kept sleeping. She peered out the window. A group of unruly men packed in a car. Eventually the car drove off without Franco.

Later that afternoon, he sat at the table smoking, depressed and contemplative. Soledad sat across from him eating cereal, reading. Later he lounged on the couch in a tank top reading newspaper classifieds.

Scratching an imaginary itch. His arms. Behind his knees.

SIX

She spent that time making the apartment more livable, throwing out a bunch of crap that had piled in the time he'd lived there. Old clothes, shoes. Washing laundry and taking down pictures of naked women. She left the lamp alone because a lot of effort had gone into making those centerfolds into a lampshade.

One morning he returned stinking of gutter and booze. Sweaty, bruised. Scratched up. He had diarrhea for days and she made him tea from orange rinds like her mother had taught her. When he was better, he held her and cried and then reiterated to her how to place her fists up and how to take a hit.

"You already showed me that," Soledad said.

"Maybe you forgot." Wearing sunglasses and letting an unlit cigarette dangle from his cut lip, he showed her, looking cool and chic. But still a little dead.

At the basketball court in Patterson Park he showed her how to duck and cover before showing her a right hook, rabbit and kidney punch, and a roundhouse.

"Hit where it will do the most damage." Franco showed her. His sweat smelled like liquor.

The sky was overcast, or maybe Baltimore was just permanently dismal. Some skinny kid in a Hardee's uniform offered him dust when they left the ball court. Franco punched him out and left him sprawled out against the fence.

Sometimes his friend Jose would come to the park and give Soledad some self-defense tips. He was white Puerto Rican, skinny and tall with a puffy afro. He wore black or blue mandarin suits and had a tattoo of Bruce Lee on his forearm.

"This is a *balisong*," he showed her the most amazing knife. "It will fuck somebody up when they least expect it."

He showed her how to fight with *escrima* sticks. Showed her how an open palm to the chin could ruin anybody's day.

SEVEN

"Can't you just poison them or push them into traffic?" She asked Franco walking home from the Mexican grocery store.

"I wanna make sure the job is done," Franco said. "No crying, no nothing. Done, and you walk. They won't be missed. Don't worry or be scared, girl. When the time comes, I'm going to ask you to kill me."

She wasn't sure of that last part. A truck had blown its horn and Franco didn't repeat himself.

EIGHT

Franco's friends came and went and sometimes he had legitimate jobs. Factory work. Butcher shop. Dishwasher. His friends were all losers, coming around to get high. Soledad would sit in a corner while they passed out on the mattress after drugs and booze.

Six months in Baltimore just ruins a person. She spent as much time as she could in the library. Work was impossible to find.

One morning Soledad walked to the Mexican store for coffee and oatmeal snack cakes. Summer was leaving and fall was just a week away. There was a cold wind coming off Fells Point.

Who was up this early? Lombard St. and its transients, that's who. Kids on their way to school.

One black, one white, heading downhill toward her, grimacing. One kid pulled his hoodie over his head, zipping up. The other pulled a bandana over his face. He was the one who threw the basketball at her. It struck her face, more shock than pain. She fell backwards down the hill, choking on blood from her busted lip. Scraped the palms of her hands. Laying on her back, opened her eyes to see two boys standing over her.

"I know you," the white kid said through the bandana. "Your dad's that skinny junkie."

The boys cackled. They couldn't have been more than thirteen.

"He's gonna OD one day," the black one said.

Bandana stood over her, pulling at her waistband. "You so pretty. Show me your pussy."

Soledad got up dizzily and fell back into a wrought iron fence in front of a church. There was dog shit on her sneakers and the back of her pants.

"He'll fucking kill you," she said. She spit blood on his sneaker.

"Yeah? I don't see him nowhere." Bandana grabbed the waist of her pants and pulled her up on her feet. They pushed and shoved her, dancing around in front of the church steps. The black youth got behind her, cupping her breasts and mouth.

"Hey baby. Tell me this," Bandana said. "Why did the rubber fly across the room?"

She struggled, her screams muffled.

"It's a joke, bitch." Bandana punched her groin. "The rubber got pissed off! That's why it flew across the room. *Thaww HA!*"

Bent over in pain, she reached for the black kid's pant leg and swept him off his feet. Jose had taught her that. The kid fell back, head smashing concrete. She vaulted backwards, her head crunching Bandana's nose.

This is yours… this will be yours to keep.

The reassembled .45 was in her hand.

"What's that?" was the last thing the black kid ever said. He had a surprised, comical look when she put a bullet in his neck.

Bandana ran uphill when she shot him twice. Bottom of the spine. She turned back to the black kid and shot again. Went up to Bandana's convulsing body and shot his chest.

She skidded on dog shit going downhill, forgetting about the coffee and breakfast cake. When she got to the apartment, Franco was awake, staring at her. She dropped the gun, ran to the bathroom, and vomited into the toilet. Afterwards she sat there a long time, cradled between the wall and porcelain. Waiting to hear something.

Not like on TV. People shit their pants when they were shot. Blood looked black when it pooled on clothes and the sidewalk. The cops took forever to show up to a crime scene in the ghetto.

When Franco stumbled around the corner of the kitchen, past the curtain separating the bathroom, she told him what happened.

NINE

Twitch was the worst news in Baltimore. *Jazz Hands,* sitting there, smoking crack with Franco one afternoon. He was the one who'd triggered his habit again, Soledad discovered. The apartment was a mess. Some of her belongings went missing. Franco didn't see her enter. He shivered in the afterglow, and then fell asleep on the couch. In the darkness, Twitch made eyes at her before fading into his own chemical haze.

First time she'd seen him was rapping to himself on some corner as her and Franco approached. Twitch was Puerto Rican from Tampa. Skinny, curly black hair. Cigarette permanently stuck to his bottom lip. Tight leather jacket, Jordache jeans and pointed leather shoes. PR shoes. *PFC's. Puerto Rican fence-climbers.* Standing on the corner of Lombard, waiting, selling, *twitching.* He had a particular tick to his face, quivering with static palsy. Hands sometimes vibrated uncontrollably. Franco nicknamed him Jazz Hands. When Twitch stood and talked he looked like Michael Jackson about to moonwalk his way to a crack pipe, always animated and talking.

Those days she hadn't seen a lot of Franco. Maybe once a week, if that. From the window she would catch him going up and down Lombard, tucked into his trench coat. Once, pursued by a helicopter. He was out with Twitch a lot. The cops would come to the door looking for them, and she'd lie and tell them they were panhandling at Fells Point. Then she'd exercise before reading herself to sleep.

Franco was working but money wasn't coming in. She'd stashed away some cans and dried fruit to get them through the next few weeks. When Franco would come in, he'd sleep for several days and wake up not knowing where he was, face full of shame and guilt. He would stumble and mumble and then leave again.

From where she slept on the sofa, she had a clear view of the front door. Barely an hour into her sleep she heard the knob turn. After a struggle, the door opened. She pulled the covers up, grabbing the gun she kept under the cushion. The kitchen light came on and Franco stood there with blood all over his trench coat. His left eye had been smashed shut. There was a bloody PVC pipe in his right hand.

He caught her looking at him.

"Twitch got it," he said. Blood sprinkled on the floor. "I killed the man who did it. Better believe I did. They caught us by surprise, fucking around. Some nigger I never seen before. Thought he was going to step in and take over the block. Fuck him. I couldn't help Twitch. They shot him point blank. But I cornered that motherfucker and bashed his fucking head in. I beat him until I was sure I crushed his fucking skull."

She went to him. He grabbed her forearm with a bloody hand.

"Dead." Franco was soberer and more alert than she'd ever seen him. "Motherfucker is dead. I know he is. He broke my fucking nose and closed my eye but he's dead. Pack your shit, honey girl. We're leaving Baltimore."

Soledad leaned her head against his shoulder at the bus terminal. Their luggage consisted of a military duffle bag each, her suitcase and a sack of miscellany. She'd done pretty good with the gauze and tape she wrapped around his head and eye. They scraped some money together for the tickets.

"I look like a mummy." Franco smiled his beat up smile.

"Just like I found you when I got here." She was half-awake. "A hobo-mummy."

"Thiggy's waiting for us in New York," Franco said. "We been friends since we were kids. Big guy."

"I've met him," she said. "Big Dominican?"

"Yeah. Fat fuck. He might have work for me there. We'll find a place soon enough. I'm gonna get some credit cards under a fake name. I think I can pull it off with some of the counterfeit ID's I got."

She read *Manifesto: Three Classic Essays on How to Change the World,* and Franco napped while they waited. They boarded after 12pm. Passengers were the most miserable wayfarers in travel history, but she knew their desperation. They weren't going on some vacation. People here were escaping the city to better things. Anywhere was better than here.

The bus was stale and sweaty. Septic odor was prevalent. The three-hour trip from Baltimore to New York City became a sorrowful eight hours. A tractor trailer had jackknifed on the Jersey turnpike, leaving them sitting there for what seemed like several human lifetimes. Soledad could see NYC just out of reach, the Statue of Liberty tiny and alone between small concrete islands. When they got to Port Transit Authority in Manhattan they took escalators up to the street level.

"Where is he?" she said, in awe of the multicolored neon jewel that was 42nd Street.

"Motherfucker has no concept of time," Franco said. He paced, angry for a fix.

When Thiago finally arrived, he parked his jalopy in the no parking zone, flashers on, and rushed out to hug them. All apologies, embracing Franco and pinching her cheeks. He was oily and smelled like burning chemicals, wearing cutoff shorts, a maroon sweat suit jacket, and tea-shades. He was buzzing with hyper energy, storing their luggage in the backseat of his blue Chrysler.

"Got some shit in the trunk," Thiago winked at Franco.

He peeled out and got on the Expressway. Soledad sat on several layers of fast food wrappers in the backseat, pressed up against their luggage.

"Damn son, they fucked you up," Thiago said.

Franco sat on the passenger side. "I killed the other guy."

"*Word?*"

Franco nodded.

They shared a junkie's laugh.

"You want hamburgers?" Thiago spoke to Soledad like a child. His eyes frequently left the road. Sometimes he drove on the breakdown lane.

"Right now, I'll eat anything," Soledad said.

New York's neon castles mesmerized her. Sparkling brighter than she remembered from her childhood visits. The sunset made it look like the evening sky was melting.

"Well, old lady's cooking some up right now," Thiago said. "But your dad and me, we gotta do this *thing*."

He handed Franco some pills and they both wired up on their way to Queens. They parked in front of a big white building. Stenciled haphazardly over the front entrance was the name **The Queen of Clubs**.

The car interior was silent, windows rolled up tight. Soledad had to pee. Franco and Thiago went into the club. Several minutes later there was shouting and shooting inside, and then they both calmly walked back out to the car. Thiago drove them south to Brooklyn.

His apartment was on Baltic St. across from the projects in Gowanus. His wife at the time was a tall and slim white woman, Italian, glasses, always wearing a teal-colored kimono.

Soledad sat in their tiny living room staring at a large color TV that played Johnny Carson reruns, eating a fat greasy hamburger between white bread. It revived her.

Thiago and Franco went out every night.

Petty crimes. Credit card fraud. Stupid things. Shoplifting groceries from Pathmark. Franco brought back ten sirloins he'd tucked into his pants. They ate steak all week. Soledad figured out several ways to prepare them and came up with creative ways to make potatoes to go with it. Thiago's wife helped out. She didn't say much, and when she wasn't in the kitchen she was locked in their bedroom reading magazines.

One afternoon Soledad was cooking and watched Franco and Thiago take the neighbor's AC unit from their window to go hock it. Franco and her spent the next few weeks living there until they were able to move into a local shelter. Soledad spent the beginning of fall at the Prospect Park library researching colleges and working on scholarships.

TEN

A homeless shelter in the East Village became their temporary home until they could get a small place of their own. The city construction was rapidly changing. Rent was inhumane. The shelter was clean, people were nice. They had a small library with tons of books. Soledad plowed through them in no time.

The kitchen kept them well-fed. Three squares a day and the coffee wasn't bad. Franco became the pride of the home, helping in the kitchen and doing maintenance work around the place. He'd cleaned up some. Moved to drinking instead of chemicals. But he did it outside the shelter to avoid eviction.

Thiago would visit, coming in with the usual con. So much so he'd convinced *himself* of everything he said. It was amusing to watch how animated his face became, eating his own bullshit by the shovelful. Thiago had Franco running all over the place for chump change.

Franco eventually saved enough money that they could finally leave the shelter. His jobs with Thiago had changed, beyond theft into collections and "cleaning up". An apartment in Spanish Harlem became available. Driving up there, the cab they rode in got a flat. Franco got into a fight with the cabby because Franco yelled at him and the cabby called him a spic. After Franco worked him over their fare was free but they had to walk the rest of the way.

"I wish your mother was here," Franco told her one day after they'd settled in. "I still love her. I know she hasn't been much to you, but you should love her too. Love your ancestors. You are their reincarnation."

Soledad nodded.

They sat on the couch they'd found on the curb. His eyes were glossy. She didn't know whether he was high, drunk or just sad. He told her about his history, growing up in the Bronx. Her mother's history. How they met in Florida, not in Japan. Her family had disowned her because she'd moved to America to study and then left school and became an addict. And then married a non-white American. Franco also told her other truths about her mother that should never be told.

But Franco never talked about the war in the desert. In retrospect, had he talked it out, loosened the memories and gotten them all out, it might have saved his life.

ELEVEN

Brooklyn shipyards. The ocean smashed a weak wooden pier and Soledad stood at its soggy edge. Across the water Manhattan looked like a prehistoric spaceship that had crash landed and assimilated the landscape. Glowing, sparkling, lines of cars moved through it like mechanized blood cells.

She didn't hate the city. New York City's primordial energy acclimated her to it, like it had been *her* city all along. New York City current had a will to disintegration. It could consume you if you let it. But once that current was in her, she no longer feared it. She learned how to navigate it.

TWELVE

Franco was gone for a whole week. Same shit, different city. One day as she left the building toward the corner, Thiago pulled up in a brand-new car and Franco was in the passenger seat.

"¡*Mira!*" Franco whistled. She tucked her hands in her jeans and walked over where Thiago double parked.

"*Nena*, we're going to Far Rockaway," Thiago said.

Franco winked. Both were high as hell. The car stunk of chemical smoke.

"Come on, mama." Franco said and opened the rear passenger door so she could climb in.

The expressway was clogged. When they got there it was dark. The neighborhood looked like it had survived a blitzkrieg. Just barely. Destination was a pool hall near Fulton and Rockaway. It stood on its own between a gas station and discotheque that had closed down in 1988. Lots of Jamaicans at the pool hall.

"Damn," Thiago said. "Some of the greasiest niggas I ever seen."

Nobody got knifed or shot that night. Franco had walked in with his arm around Soledad. They talked to a man named Mantler. He gave them money, but their business wasn't clear.

Then a very long drive to Staten Island, the forgotten sister borough.

Shootings and stabbings were just the peripherals of the city, the core savagery before the massive cleanup which would eventually choke out the natives. Another night some weeks later in the Bronx, she watched Thiago throw a Molotov cocktail at a car that passed by. Five black youths were riding inside. Competition that had to be eliminated. Thiago, light skin but passed for black, and from the islands, made a joke about, *"You know how rum is made? Set fire to they ass and melt them niggas down! Gonna trickle out the muffler. Grab a shot glass."*

She'd never heard the two of them laugh so hard.

THIRTEEN

Thiago had moved into a small office above a funeral home. He was eating pizza, sucking his greasy thumbs.

"She'll be creeping when you least expect her." he said. "Them round eyes, they trick you. Look at her. You wouldn't know her mom's a Jap. I mean you can see it, but she keeps you guessing. Shit, they just see a girl walk up, they not expecting she's carrying a piece. This is a good thing. You done good, Franco."

Pretending to sleep on the lobby couch, Soledad heard them through the floor vent.

"But if she get caught," Thiago said. "Same rules apply."

"It's gonna be hard to convince her," said Franco. "I don't think she'll want to do it."

Thiago licked all his fingers. "No matter. She'll come around to it. Hey, you got Robo Ray?"

"I think so."

"What about the Bronx Bomber?"

"Probably."

"Probably? You're fucking up, bro. Either you did or didn't."

FOURTEEN

Strange men, *illegitimate men*, moved past her up the stairs to Thiago's office. White men, but not cops. Black suits and ties, sunglasses and little wires wrapped around their ears, carrying laptops and briefcases.

When they were gone, Thiago waved her into the office. He joked that she might need a gun for each hand.

"Them shits cost a lot, though," Thiago had said. "But you'd look hot, coming out of an elevator with a gat in each hand, all slo-mo and shit…"

"It doesn't work like that." Soledad had said.

"I know. Do it hood-rat style. In and out. *Pow-pow!*"

Part III: The Rip

ONE

Students began occupying the streets, corporate lobbies, and had sit ins at the campus. Myriad faces, genders, colors and cultures. Sitting on the floor discussing communism, capitalism, occupying, protesting, etc. Sharing stories of arrests and beatings at the hands of cops, counter protests by racist white people. Dialogue about politics, Marxism, neo-capitalism. Soledad sat among them.

A student named Ana, wearing a military jacket handed out flyers. Soledad went out with her for coffee after the gathering. She was a tall half-Korean, half-black girl wearing big eyeglasses, ring in her nose, tattoos, and hoop earrings. She smelled like rosewater and pot.

"If there is no revolt, then it's all just theater," Ana said. "There's no change without a wakeup call to the bourgeoisie. That's all *we're* saying. That's what the movement is about."

"Yeah, but what do you have left after that? What comes next?" said Soledad. "You still wind up conforming to a new kind of status that's basically a version of the old one. *The new bourgeoisie*. Same lameness. No permanent change. Not without a real breakthrough. You have to go at it with a hammer, breaking everything you've ever embraced. All your old thought processes have to be dismantled. *Smashed*."

"There'll be reformation," Ana said.

"I'm talking extreme measures." Soledad's coffee had gone cold.

"You mean like setting off a bomb?" Ana said.

"That's urban terrorism."

A male friend of theirs came by and sat with them. Dressed in black, wearing eye and lip makeup and multicolored hair.

"Speaking of bombs," he said. "Imagine if you will, how Hiroshima changed things. It brought peace to an imperialist country. So was it really so horrible?"

Soledad ignored him. Ana rolled her eyes at him.

"Makes no sense," Ana said. "Plus… God…*no*. That's *extremism*."

"I mean, the change begins in our way of acting or thinking and living," Soledad said. "Not just holding signs or getting the shit kicked out of you by the cops. This isn't Berkley in the fucking '60's."

Ana caressed her coffee cup. She looked off to the side so as not to look Soledad in the eyes. They were dark and ireful.

"That's too radical," Ana said. "I mean, I feel you. I really do. Not for our group. This is grassroots, from the ground up. Peace and petitions. Protesting and voting. We're trying to build a more peaceable society."

Soledad smiled. "Malcolm said, *by any means necessary*."

"Malcolm is dead," the male student said.

Soledad looked at him. She pointed a finger gun at him. *"Pew,"* she said. "You have to manifest what you want society to become. You can revolt all you want. You'll still wind up with dystopia. To start anew you must rebuild a foundation, not build on top of the old shit that crumbled."

"I feel you," Ana said, drumming her fingers. "What matters is if the impact leaves an impression. That impression is where the change happens. Impact from petitions, meetings, be-ins and protests."

Soledad disagreed. "I'm curious as to what the leftovers would look like."

"The end-results?" said Ana.

"Yes. History shows that peace-loving hippies grew up to be money-hungry yuppies. What's going to become of *this* generation? What dystopia will they establish for themselves after their 'revolution'? I think these people who are occupying are doing it just to get noticed and have a good time. I don't know that there's anything good coming out of it. They're on the brink of rioting mostly. Cops kick a few people around. Then everyone goes home with some sense of satisfaction without there being any actual change."

"But who's saying anything on their behalf?" Ana said. "If no one else is speaking for *them*, who's really talking about the disenfranchised? Who's down in the trenches to voice how pissed off *we* are? Nobody else is doing it."

"You're talking sitting in and I'm talking violence. But in the end, there must be a revolution in the head. Anything else is just a riot. For the sake of civil disturbance. To hangout."

"So, what you're saying," the male student said. "What she's saying is bourgeoisie begets bourgeoisie."

Soledad pointed the finger at him again, this time she wasn't thinking about shooting him.

TWO

Later, they continued the conversation in Ana's dorm.

"I get the feeling you're not feeling the cause," Ana said, smoking weed from an apple.

"Cause?" Soledad leaned against the kitchenette countertop. She passed on the smoke. "I'm for the *ideal.* Marxism works on paper, but I don't want what's yours. I want my own. I don't ask for a lot. But I'm not going to share everything that's mine. Everything I've worked for. That's not my mindset. I'm not a joiner."

"You'll find that when you have it all you don't really need it," Ana said.

"Says the privileged girl from Rochester."

"Hey, at the end of the day, it's a fucking class struggle," Ana said. "I've realized that. And you know all about that. So what, just be free-falling anarchists? If we're going to maintain tribes, we need guidelines to make them work. Can't just have people showing up and changing shit to fit their script. I mean, what are you looking forward to after graduation? I'm staying with the cause, through and through."

Soledad sighed. "The cause is going to change by the time we're out there." She paced the dormitory, arms crossed. "What do you really think will be waiting for us?"

THREE

Soledad walked the backstreets of Spanish Harlem back home. The city transformed day by day. It wasn't so much in the architecture, but the people and the type of commerce they demanded. Got to where the bodegas were selling fancy beer and health food items.

Walking into the apartment's unlit vacuum gave her the feeling of entering a void, a black hole's negative space.

There'd been nights when she'd played checkers with Franco on the small throw rug she'd bought on Canal St. Then tossing and turning on the sofa, trying to sleep while he watched TV at full volume. Or staying up late reading while Franco watched some horror movie when they used to broadcast them late night.

She slept on the sofa still, even if the room and bed were available. At this point she'd learned to sleep anywhere. Looking into the apartment's void she remembered Franco sleeping on the floor, shivering with junk sickness. Finding him sick and vomiting in the bathroom when he went cold turkey and made a mess of it. From that point on he started to drink enough for five people.

From a window she saw Franco's ghost in the street, shaking hands with unscrupulous types. He would haunt Spanish Harlem long after she moved out.

Morning faded in slowly. She'd managed a full night of sleep for once. The city's cacophony began early in the morning. Commuters, honking cars, trucks backing up and unloading. Sirens. Whistling. Always someone whistling at someone else. Taxis blaring their horns and the sun hitting her in the face through the window, reminding her she didn't live in a box. That she walked this ball of dirt every day as it circled that globe of radioactive light.

Even in the morning, she could see Franco still lying there. Snoring. Bandaged. People honking for him to come downstairs. She heard the echo of them calling his name.

Soledad would stumble off the sofa to shake him, but he wouldn't wake up. He rolled over on the throw rug and kept sleeping. She looked out the window, seeing Thiggy Biggs in his fancy new car packed with a group of unruly men. Eventually they drove off without Franco.

Memories fortified by her still living here, still seeing his furniture, his things. Smelling his presence. Seeing the empty bottles of vodka. Finding the occasional needle.

She made coffee and sipped it, staring out the window. She couldn't come around to sit at the table any longer. She could still see Franco there smoking, depressed and contemplative. His image burned into the wall.

Franco on the sofa reading classifieds. Scratching an imaginary itch. Behind his arms, behind his knees. Between his toes.

FOUR

Those last days, when Franco no longer wore bandages. Soledad read a textbook as they walked side by side. They found a spot on a bench and enjoyed the morning. Central Park was a secret, magical place to forget the metal and steel fort that was Manhattan. The sun was a bright radioactive bloom. They spent the day together with her knowing his sobriety was short lived. Later, back at the apartment, he'd fallen asleep on the couch watching TV.

Next day Soledad woke up, got out of bed, and searched the apartment. Franco wasn't there. She looked out the window. On the corner facing the park, Franco was waiting for the man. Shortly after, a lone street hippie showed up, also waiting. One of his hands was bandaged. Franco and the hippie nodded to each other but were cautious of each other.

"You got the time?" Franco said.

"Sold my watch, man. Sorry," the ragged hippie said.

Franco shrugged. "Waiting on a friend."

"Sure, man," the hippie chuckled. "Itchy and patient. I'm waiting on the saucers to take me back home. Ha ha. Most days I'm just waiting for the next bus to take me outta here. Hate this fucking place. Hate what it's becoming. Just wanna close my eyes, count one-two-three, disappear and never come back."

"Where you from?" said Franco.

"Nowhere, man. Been floating city to city. Following the Dead."

"Huh. Grateful Dead? I thought they broke up."

The hippie was fidgety and twitchy. "You thought the Dead were dead? Nah, man. Well, *Jerry's* dead. I ain't seen them in a long while. Guess I never came to terms with his death. Hit everybody hard. The scene ain't been the same, though. It's all commercialized, t-shirts, beer, sponsorship. I been drifting around since. Alls I know is that I once saw the Dead play 'Space' back at RFK for like three hours. It removed me from this existence and I ain't looked back since."

"What happened to your hand?" Franco said. He found a half-spent butt and picked it up. The hippie gave him a light and they shared it.

"You meet all kinds of strangers on the road, man," the hippie said.

"Streets are mean," Franco said. "Sometimes you gotta protect yourself." The hippie said. He lifted his bad hand. "Shit happens. I see you, though. You're not really here either. You're gone. Like someone is in your house dreaming you."

Franco felt the itch a little more. He scratched and leaned, looking down the street as if the man was a late bus arriving.

"Hey man," the hippie said. "You wanna just get the fuck out of here after the score? I gotta place we can smoke a little something."

"Uh, yeah." Franco scratched his neck.

The man arrived. Some hooded dude named Grinch. Handshake drugs traded and he was ghost.

"Aw, man. Let's do this." The hippie said. "This'll loosen you up. I remember that guy that sold us this. Used to meet up with him at the Island of Coney. They don't let transients on that beach no more so I moved inland."

"You're far from home, brother." Franco followed.

"I went around, following a Dead caravan and but got stranded." The hippie reached into his back pocket for a bottle of cough syrup and took a few small sips before offering some to Franco.

"I know what you mean." Franco sipped and walked. "I been stranded in this fucking city a long time. Like I'm imprisoned here."

"That's a bummer, man," the hippie said. "Well, I'm literally stranded here. Busted hand, live in a garbage can, always waiting for the man."

The hippie's place was a storage shed behind the Mudanza Moving Co. that he'd broken into. A shack with a bucket in the corner and a few milk crates to sit on. There was an old bench seat against the plywood wall. Crushed cigarette packs, cinnamon bun wrappers and other garbage strewn on the floor.

"That used to be part of my car," the hippie pointed at the bench seat. "1969 Chevy Nova. Can't afford no car in this city, no sir. This is where I sleep."

Franco showed him how to improvise a soda can into a smoking vessel. They sat on the bench seat, lighting up. Whatever they smoked looked like magical crystals.

"I'm gonna let you in on a secret," the hippie said.

"What, this is your mother's place?" Franco cracked and they had a good laugh.

"Shh, listen. I only tell this to people I trust. *What's your name?*"

"P-Pablo," Franco said.

"Nice, like *Picasso*." The hippie giggled. "Listen, I got schematics for this time machine I'm building. I don't want to talk about it in detail right now. *They* might be listening. If I had it working or had the ability to go back in time... *dooood.* All the concerts I would go see, man! All those dead rock stars. Garcia. The Doors. Hendrix. Dude, at Woodstock, how many hits of acid you think Hendrix took? I've studied that movie carefully. Many times. When he's playing the American anthem. Slipped it under his wristband. *Bam.* One hit, each arm. He kept blotter under his bands. He had a razor slit on his forehead that he used to dose into. That's why he wore a headband all the time. I know. I saw him. He lifts his arm after he strums upward and takes a hit. *Pow,* another one. Those are the secrets I want to tap into, man. You got me? *Elevation.*"

They smoked some more. The storage room took on an ethereal but toxic vibe. The walls vibrated, the air got thick and heavy. Everything was hazy and blurry.

FIVE

In a low-lit office, a well-dressed Thiago let Franco visit. Old buddy, Thiago. Thiggy Biggs. He'd been the one to get away with it and come out shiny. Gold rings, necklace, diamond on his pinky, diamond on his left lateral incisor. Polished dome. If he was any sort of charm, it was an unlucky one. At least for Franco.

Next to Thiago sat Leo Kern. Thin man in a black suit and tie. Didn't say much but oversaw everything that was happening. Thiago looked nervous whenever this man was around.

Soledad sat on the leather wingback to the right of Thiago's desk reading her copy of *Rules for Radicals* by Saul D. Alinsky.

Franco waited his turn, standing in front of the desk. Thiago shook his hand. They embraced. Franco pulled up a chair and sat. They vacillated on sports and food. Nearby bodegas, which Chinese joints had the best fried chicken.

"Been a minute, *mano*," Thiago said.

Kern lurked in the shadows. He stared at Soledad.

"Who beat your ass?" Thiago asked Franco. "You back to dating Puerto Ricans? What I tell you?"

Franco laughed nervously. He looked like shit and knew it. Soledad saw the chasm widening between these two blood brothers.

Thiago looked at Soledad. "Look at that beauty.

Takes after her mom, obviously." Franco laughed nervously.

"Muthafucka, you bumming rides off garbage trucks again?" Thiago said.

Franco's smile hid his embarrassment.

"Didn't the VA put a metal plate in your head?"

Franco nodded.

Thiago laughed. "It evened out that ape skull of yours."

They laughed again. Even Kern chuckled.

"You here for a handout?" Thiago's diamond tooth gleamed.

Franco cleared his throat. "I'd never ask you like that, brotha. I'm here for work. Looking for heavy stuff to do. But I can't pass a drug test to earn a lousy penny."

"My man," Thiago said. "Get piss from someone who's clean. Put it in a rubber when you go take a piss test. You gonna work in a bank? Even with clean piss, who's gonna hire a bum like you?"

"Man, even the shit jobs want clean piss," Franco said. "And the VA ain't gonna do shit for me."

"My man, I did what I could," Thiago said. "It ain't all the VA's fault."

"I'm struggling, man. I can't do shit. 'Specially if they say I'm unstable."

"VA said that?"

"Yeah."

"Not like you have a choice then. You really that crazy? PTSD fucking witchoo? That war was like ten years ago."

"Fuck that shit. I'm fine," Franco said. "I'm hungry and I got a daughter to support."

"We've had this conversation, homie," Thiago said. "What about the warehouse gig? Supervisor said you haven't been back in like three weeks. You have to show up to get paid, nigga. That's how it works."

"Come on, man. I'm better than that. What do you need done around *here*?"

Thiago looked at his empty cup.

"Right now, I need some coffee." Thiago laughed. "I need my spreadsheets updated accurately. Number crunching. My Cadi needs a wash. I need a blowjob." He looked at Soledad. "Whatchoo want, Franco? Wanna clean my toilets? There's plenty of puke to clean off on the weekends at the pool hall."

"You bought the place from the Jamaicans?"

"Took it," Thiago said. "In my drive to diversify, I took that shit from them. I'll prolly let it go to shit and sell it for upscale housing."

"Pfft," Franco said. "In Far Rockaway?"

"You'd be surprised the money coming into this borough and what *they* got planned for it."

"Come on, *hermano*," Franco said. "Like the old days."

"Look brother, I appreciate the work we did together," Thiago said. "I wouldn't be here without your help. We ain't kids no more. Ain't no more stickup work around here. I got people in places doing what they doing. People who haven't let me down."

"Fuck you, man," Franco said. "I stuck around through all that bullshit. Whatta ya got? Freight action? Hustling AC units? Stealing shit from the back of Pathmark?"

"I don't roll like dat no more, my man," Thiago said. "In case you didn't know, a lot of shit's changed. I have evolved. *Diversified.* The business has up-scaled, if you feel me."

Franco waved a dismissive hand at him.

"Bah. I don't fucking believe that for one minute," he said. "You ain't turned a trick out or robbed somebody since back then? Your dick is limp, man. We was still rolling muthafuckas last year, when it suited you."

Thiago laughed.

"You muthafucka," Thiago said. "Don't say that shit around anybody else, hear me?" He leaned over and whispered, "I rolled this white dude a few weeks ago. Watched him for days, going in and out of his apartment. I got right into it. Wore a ski mask and shit. Held him up with my old 9 while he was getting in his car. Just to see if I could still do it. And I did it. But that's all petty shit. As you can probably tell, I'm playing with some big boys now." He gestured his surroundings. "Managing new things."

"Right," Franco said. "That's what I mean. I want in with the big dogs. I know you. I know how far you came. You my gateway, Thiggy. Don't hold out on me, man."

Thiago massaged his meaty forehead. "I don't owe you a fucking thing, bro. I don't know what you think I got going on here. I got you the warehouse job. And you blew it. I mean, I wasn't gonna leave you in there to rot forever. But you gotta show me you can keep up, man. I got people for this other stuff. I'm not about to put a junkie knot-head at the back of a truck or making collection runs."

Franco leaned back, hand at his heart. "That hurts me, brother."

"Well, don't come in here all high and mighty, muthafucka. Don't ever accuse me of not being real. I passed you the rock multiple times, so don't give me that bullshit."

"Come on, man," Franco said. "Dirty laundry. Let me handle it. I need real fucking work. Get me in the network."

"Can you drive?" Thiago said.

"Not fit to drive." Franco folded his arms. "Per the VA. Those motherfuckers don't know shit, man."

Thiago scoffed. "There's no bullshitting around it: I got dirty work. There's *always* dirty work. I don't mean cleaning the toilets neither. I mean, if that's what you really want. How's your good hand?"

Franco hesitated but slowly raised his right hand.

"Steady as ever," he said.

"You blew up a lot of shit in that sandbox, right? You know your way around demolition? Explosives?"

"A lot of shit blew up around me." Franco tensed up. "You know where I been, Thig. Shooting *hajis* was mostly target practice."

"This is *seriously* dirty work, my man. Not that hoodie shit we used to pull off. Pop, pop, drop and run." Thiago rapped his knuckles on the table. "Let's talk details soon, okay? I'll let you know. Can I call you?"

"Got no phone," Franco said.

Thiago looked at him sideways. "Jesus, man. You living mad niggerish. How you 'spect her to talk to her friends? How's she talk to boys? Damn. All right. Leo here will come for you."

Franco told him their current address. Kern didn't write it down, but he nodded.

Thiago told Franco,

"Now, when we come calling, don't just roll over and keep sleeping, muthafucka. I'm working out some construction deals. Big money. Shit. Just the government contracts alone will keep me busy for years. Union shit. There's always delays with that, but it never stops the bankroll. Even if we do nothing, the checks keep coming. Ain't Uncle Sam grand?"

"Maybe I'll make foreman." Franco smiled. His teeth were crooked and gray.

"Oh, you ain't working my construction jobs. Trust me." Thiago dismissed them.

Franco and Soledad waved on their way out. Kern leaned in, whispering into Thiago's ear.

SIX

Days passed and Franco was called down, then driven to an office where Leo Kern showed him photos he kept of people he'd killed. And pictures of people they were going to kill. He showed Franco a few guns inside an old suitcase, gave him a few pointers. Franco looked paltry and sick compared to the slick, devilish Kern.

Later they drove to a dingy apartment building on 147th. Daytime. Long, dark hallway. Garbage everywhere, graffiti covering everything. The smell of old fried food, piss, and the general aura of neglect. Franco knocked on the last door at the end of the hall. A dazed man opened the door, wearing only boxer shorts, smoking a cigarette.

Franco knew this man, only because he'd once seen him make some sort of business transaction with Thiago. The man had slipped an envelope to Thiago and that had been the last time Franco had seen him until now.

The man looked at Franco and before he could ask, he realized there was a gun aimed at him. Franco pulled the trigger.

SEVEN

There were videos for rent at the back of the store. Local rapper, Revolt, was in the rear checking out bootleg Kung Fu tapes on the back shelf.

"My man," he went up to one of the counter people. "You know if you got *One-Armed Swordsman*?"

The man behind the counter acknowledged him and went under the counter. He grabbed a video tape from there and handed it to him.

"Ah, okay." Revolt said. "This ain't it, chief. I got this one. *Shogun Assassin*. Yeah, that's hot. Watched it plenty, nameen. Listen, c'mere."

Revolt sat on a foot stool. Bahia and Iberia products pressed against his back. Red beans, black beans, pink beans. Corn, canned beets, canned green beans, etc.

"I grew up with these," he told the man while holding a stack of videos. "Like, you know, for a young brother, there was nothing to relate to on TV. *Sanford and Son*, maybe. *Good Times*. *What's Happening?* Otherwise we'd spend the afternoons after school watching kung fu flicks, nameen? Then we'd make our own costumes and jump around like karate masters and shit. Go down to Chinatown and buy them kung fu slippers and Mandarin jackets."

The man understood him and nodded. They didn't speak the same language but were on the same page. The man helped him peruse the shelf for the elusive *One-Armed Swordsman* while Revolt chitchatted.

Soledad entered the bodega. This was after Franco had died.

"S'up, shawty," Revolt said, and she turned to him, curiously. "You Franco's girl, ain't you?"

Soledad nodded. Not shyly but closed off. "Be blessed, sorry about your pops."

She managed a smile. "Thank you."

After picking up a few basic items, she went to pay. The owner spoke Spanish to other customers.

"*Que tal,*" the man said. "*¿Hija de Franco?*"

Soledad nodded. "*Si.*"

"*Vas a pagar o credito?*"

"Um, I have cash," she said.

"*O, si. Cash es bueno. Pero Franco tiene una lista de credito por dos meses.*"

"I'm sorry. I don't really speak Spanish."

"He says you have credit here. Your father paid it in advance. Before his demise." Leo Kern stood behind her. He wore a basic black suit, white shirt and black tie. Sunglasses. Gray snakeskin boots. He grabbed some gum and slapped a $5 bill on the wooden counter. The man put his hand on it and Kern poked it with his finger. He looked at the man. The man made a serious face but nodded. He pulled back the money nervously.

She completed the transaction without having to pay.

"You don't speak Spanish?" Kern said.

"I studied it in school, but didn't retain it," Soledad said without looking at him. He loomed over her, breathing over her.

"Surprising that in a country where over three hundred languages are spoken, everyone just wants to speak English," he said.

"They can speak whatever the fuck they want." Soledad grabbed the paper bag of groceries and left.

"That's everything?" Kern opened the door for her. She smelled mint on his breath and Old Spice on his neck.

"You're the man who works for Thiago." She said, walking. She looked over her shoulder briefly and said, "Tell him I said fuck off."

Kern nodded, still standing inside the store.

EIGHT

Franco's partnership with Kern had him wearing suits bought and tailored on Canal St. Franco would sleep in them, so they always looked like wrinkled, skid row chic.

He sat quietly watching TV when Soledad came out of the bathroom, drying her hair. He got up almost immediately and left the apartment.

"Meeting a friend," he said. Unshaven, bloodshot eyes about to burst from his face. The usual. But with new clothes.

Hours later he'd stumbled back into the apartment, waking her up. He got sick in the bathroom, and came out bare-chested, holding a gun. Hands shaking.

"I couldn't do it." Franco said, confused junk-zombie, droning aimlessly around the living room. "These hands. I can't get them to stop shaking. These worthless fucking hands. It's never happened before. If I can't do this... I can't let Thiago down again. I can't."

NINE

Her savings dwindled. A cut off notice appeared on the door. She had a discussion with Franco, and he promised to get some money and make the payment. Said he'd drop it off by hand. He did eventually, but there was never enough. Not with it mostly going in his veins or up in smoke.

TEN

Unknown apartment. Kern and Franco forced their way in. The apartment was already ransacked like a junkie's way station. No dialogue. Money collected so there was no need to kill anyone.

On to the next job. The Bronx.

Franco sat on the sofa there, high, drowsy. He looked over to see Kern across from him in the bathroom, sitting on the toilet lid. There was a man on the floor tied up. Kern was talking but it was all muffled. Kern bounced a handball he'd found on the floor. He shoved the ball into the man's mouth and closed the bathroom door. Franco blinked and passed out. He woke up in the passenger seat of Kern's car. Awake but heavy-eyed.

ELEVEN

Soledad spared $5 to spend at the café. Ana arrived dressed more conservatively than two semesters ago. Her hair was longer. She wore makeup fresh from the salon. Nails too. Soledad was lucky to have washed her outfit the previous night. Jeans and a button shirt. They embraced. Ana kissed her cheek.

"You haven't been back to finish?" Ana said.

"Trying to get another grant." Soledad lied.

They ordered coffee. Ana seemed to be humoring the surroundings. She talked mostly about her boyfriend, his business. They were talking about raising children and moving to Vermont. Soledad barely got a word in. Not that she would share any of her real life with Ana. But once upon a time they'd discussed the pros and cons of hurling Molotovs through a police precinct window.

"I haven't seen you on campus much," Ana said.

"*Just looking after my dad, while he's sick.*" was the one true thing Soledad said. "Don't have money right now."

"What about another loan?" Ana said.

"I got other priorities," Soledad said. "My dad needs me a lot these days."

"His PTSD?"

"Yeah."

"I'm sorry," Ana said. Soledad noticed how her cheeks looked fuller, plump from whatever it was that she pumped into her face to make them fuller.

"I couldn't bring Troy along," Ana said. "He's so busy. Oh my god, I was planning his birthday party and it was supposed to be a surprise? I blew it because when I sent out the email invite not only did everybody receive it, he did too! Ha ha. *I'm so stupid.*

Okay, so we got a dog? Oh my god, he's like our child. You wouldn't believe how much work he is to care for. We went on vacation and had such a hard time finding somebody to take care of him..."

Made Soledad think of dog fights. Dead dogs.

TWELVE

Ana's voice had echoed in Soledad's head as she considered where Franco might have been that afternoon.

Back alleys in the daytime, gunshots ringing from the buildings around him. Franco came out running and got in Kern's car. Blocks away they disposed of the hot, smoking piece.

Kern handed him his wad of cash. They drove to see a man who deposited small baggies of poison into Franco's hand. Kern drove him to the building on 5th and double parked with the emergencies flashing. He slapped Franco out of his stupor, then pushed him on the sidewalk and left him there.

THIRTEEN

Walking back from meeting Ana she got lost. New York City was a maze that could eat a girl alive. The streets opened and closed like interdimensional portals. Construction wasn't always the cause, though often the streets looked refabricated with each passing. Too many potholes to fix. Too easy to fall into them.

The East Broadway station was closed so she walked to West 4th St. but turned out the F line was down for repairs. She could have taken an express, but she hated the bus more than the train. She sauntered Lower Manhattan.

The city folded and transformed with every passing block. Gentrification created islands of exclusion. Some locations were familiar from their historical significance. Effigies before their dismantling, like The Knitting Factory before it relocated to Brooklyn; CBGB and The Bottom Line. Too many pizzerias, bookstores, head shops and bars to name. She knew their era had long passed by the number of leasing billboards covering up graffiti.

The streets angled and narrowed southward. That's how she knew where she was without the Twin Tower beacons. She was the last person on earth.

She made it to the corner of Canal St. and 6th. Avenue of the Americas. Parking garages and business offices. The only vehicle on the street was a parked moving truck, flashers blinking. She heard chanting. Singing voices coming from inside the truck. Female voices. Singing a Bob Marley song. She heard the backdoor of the truck roll open and turned to see several women jump down, wearing military green, orange or blue jumpsuits. She overheard their conversations. Talk of marches. Acquiring guns. Women discussing the coming of a socialist age. She crossed while they gathered in the street. Someone handed down picket signs from inside the truck.

Soledad came back the next day to the same spot. She stood on the same corner sure this was the place. There was no parked truck nor its passengers, not a sign that there had even been a gathering.

FOURTEEN

Took Soledad all day to get back from the trip, which included an afternoon class at Marymount. Made it back at sunset. Just in time to meet Franco stepping off the elevator. He wore one of those wrinkled suits with the tie all loose. They walked side by side, north on 6th Ave. He hadn't worked in a week. Not that she'd seen, anyway.

Told her he wanted either fried chicken or Chinese food for dinner. She worried less when he was hungry for food.

Scaffolding, plywood boards, coming soon posters prefaced the neighborhood's slow makeover. Changes had come to Harlem Cho's where they picked food up. More white people getting takeaway. Slumming in poor 'hoods because the food was better. The takeaway was a righteous risk when picking up cocaine along the way.

Franco left her in the dining room, walking into the kitchen. Soledad ordered eggrolls and settled in a small table tucked in the corner. The odd wallflower, she drank from a crinkly water bottle while reading a Bolaño paperback. The food here was highly saliferous. She nursed a second bottle.

Franco was gone longer than usual.

She'd lost track of time when in entered two slumming Jersey-girls about her age.

"*Stacy*, girl: where'd you those nails?" Blaise said. "And *when*? That's like the first I've seen them."

"At that Tahitian place," Stacy said. "I totally forgot to show you."

"Oh my god."

"Babe. It's in Midtown."

"I thought they were Korean," Blaise said.

"I wasn't paying attention," Stacy said. "They all look the same to me." Her phone rang. She looked at the screen but didn't flip it open. She silenced it. "He keeps calling me. He drunk-dialed me last night."

They stood with their backs to the counter and brightly lit menu.

"I told you not to fuck him," Stacy said. "You fuck before you're in relationship status and that always fucks everything up. He's such a jerk. Don't answer his calls anymore."

"Whatever," Blaise said.

Stacy rolled her eyes. "He fucks you once and thinks he can just keep coming back with no strings attached? No, girl. You keep that door open, and he'll keep using you."

Blaise looked at her phone, contemplating.

"He's so big," she said. "I can't help myself."

"That's just an illusion," Stacy said. "Don't get dick blind about it. The only thing that makes it look that thick is his foreskin 'cause he ain't circumcised."

"How do you know?" said Blaise.

"C'mon, who hasn't seen that thing?"

"Shh. Not so loud. There's people here."

"You gonna order something?"

"Ew, I don't know," Blaise said. Then she whispered, "*I just want some coke…*"

"Shh," Stacy said. "Like, who's gonna hear? That gypsy girl over there?"

They giggled and the conversation turned to Soledad in between ordering General Tso's chicken and egg foo young. And asking if they could buy an "extra Coke."

"Gypsy?" Stacy said popping open a diet soda. "She looks Muslim or something."

"Like a terrorist?" Blaise ate. Sauce stained her fresh manicure. "Don't they wrap up their heads and faces?"

"I guess. I don't know," Stacy said.

"Where's Rachel?" Blaise craned her head, looking outside.

"Fuck her," Stacy said. She looked at her phone, flipped it open and responded to a text message.

"Again?" said Blaise. "You guys are like on the third cycle of your feud. Is there a time when you're *not* bickering?"

"I asked her to come out but she's usually too busy fucking my boyfriend. We're not talking right now."

Blaise considered what she'd just heard.

"Well, shit," Blaise said. "Just throw a party and get over it. Kiss clams and make up. But, girl, you know she's gotta have the clap. There's no way she can be doing all those random guys and not have it."

"Gross," Stacy said. "That's so gross. I know she fucks a lot of random AC dudes, but I didn't know it was like that."

"You could have it too since she's fucked your boyfriend."

"Not if I just sucked his dick," Stacy said.

"Ew, um, hello? *Not true!*"

Stacy whispered,

"Did you see his new car?"

"Girl, yes. *I can't believe those ugly rims!*"

"Right? I was like, *'you nigger-lover, I can't believe you ruined your car with those!'*"

"I ain't riding in it 'til he gets rid of them," Blaise said.

"They're worth more than the whole car!" said Stacy.

"What kind of man puts those on a little piece of shit Toyota like that? Gross!"

Stacy cut her off. "Holy shit, I can't believe she's here. Look!"

Blaise saw her too. "Did you invite her?"

Stacy said, "Maybe. I told her we'd be hanging out in the City. *She just came to powder her nose.*"

Blaise gave her a heated look.

"How was I supposed to know you two were fighting?" said Stacy.

Rachel joined them and they kissed on the cheek, all fake smiles and hellos.

The first thing Rachel said was, "*Lookit my new phone.*"

"Samsung?" said Blaise.

"Fuck yeah," said Stacy.

"God, I love it," Rachel said. "Let's take a picture."

They squished together, puckered their lips and posed for their phone cameras.

"Wanna eat, *Rache*?" Blaise said.

"This place is a dump," Stacy said. "Where's my coke man? You guys wanna roll later? We should just roll."

"Molly? Ooh, no," said Rachel. "It dries up my pussy."

Blaise rolled her eyes and then nodded toward Soledad.

"Look at her," she said. "She waiting on a trick or something?"

Stacy laughed. "Who'd pay for that?"

FIFTEEN

Soledad walked out of Harlem Cho's alone. Eventually the Jersey girls stumbled out, hyper and ready to take on Manhattan like in *Sex and the City*.

They headed toward the station on Malcolm X when they immediately found themselves on their knees facing a wall. Soledad had pulled her hoodie over her head and wrapped a scarf around her face. Gun held confidently in her hand. She paced back and forth behind them, pointing it. Rachel complained about her knees. Blaise sobbed. Stacy recited lines of racist rhetoric. Soledad took their money and anything else she found of value in their purses.

SIXTEEN

Franco was not coming back tonight, lost to oblivion no doubt, in some bodega broom closet somewhere in the bowels of Spanish Harlem. He'd slipped out the back of Harlem Cho's and into the cold comfort of his drugs. Soledad walked to their apartment alone, throwing out the Jersey girls' credit cards like parade confetti, their ID's, and cell phones too. Whatever cash they had she crumbled and threw into the gutter.

SEVENTEEN

Nighttime, a week later. Out in the street. Soledad wore her hoodie, walking Franco, helping to keep him steady. They came to a seedy afterhours bar in Queens.

"Stay out here. Be my eyes while I'm inside," Franco said. "They think I'm here to score."

She waited outside. Franco told the doorman he was going to make contact, to keep an eye on his daughter.

Inside the bar the world was red and yellow, dim lamps glowing on every table and above the bar. The red velvet curtains were dusty, the hems tattered from rats chewing on them. The place hadn't been renovated since the 1980's.

Franco had been a kid back then, coming in here to buy cigarettes out of the machine, or buy firecrackers out the backdoor. Velvety gray smoke clung to the air. The music from the jukebox was hissy and tinny. The Isley Brothers. Roxy Music. Kool and the Gang.

He didn't recognize anyone. But there was the man who'd been seen talking to Thiago a few weeks back, drinking by himself at the bar. Franco stalled at the cigarette machine, same one he'd fed dollars into when he was 12. The man climbed off the stool and Franco followed him into the restroom. The man walked into a stall and pissed. Franco waited in the shadows near the paper towel box. When the man took too long, Franco pretended to use the urinal just in case anybody else walked in.

The man came out of the stall and fixed his hair in the mirror before opening the door.

"Are you Benny?" Franco said.

The man stopped. "What of it?"

"Benny," Franco said. "You wanna wash your hands?"

"What's it to you?" Benny said. "Where I come from, we ain't gottta wash our hands. We keep our business clean."

"Not even when you touch your asshole?" Franco said.

"You thinking about my asshole, faggot?"

Franco shivered, slick with sweat. His eyes widened. He said,

"You must be from New Jersey."

EIGHTEEN

Outside, Soledad sat on the bouncer's stool. She watched several bar patrons throw Franco onto the sidewalk. He wiped the blood from his mouth, moving sickly towards Soledad. She held him and they walked off to the left of the building. Rounded a corner and leaned against a graffitied wall.

"You gotta believe me, baby girl," Franco said.

"This isn't how I want it for you. I swear."

Benny walked past them on the sidewalk, stumbling toward his car. Franco followed him but was too sick to draw. The gun fell from his waistband to the ground. For a second Soledad just looked at it where it fell on the cracked sidewalk. Benny was at his car unlocking the driver door when he saw them approaching. He pulled a snubby out of his waistband, reaching over the roof of the car, shooting Franco.

He hadn't counted on Soledad springing up behind Franco, shooting back.

NINETEEN

They were in the apartment an hour later. It was late but the city was steamy and sticky. Loud and messy. Franco and Soledad stumbled in.

"You think somebody followed us?" Franco asked.

"I don't think so. We took a different train at the switch. We wound up on the A. It's empty at night. People are still out there burning down the city."

"Huh?" He said. "What's burning?"

"It's a joke. The city is hot. People are out. It's New York. What do you think?"

"I think that Thiago is yelling into a phone right now. Pissed off on how it went down. Can you call him for me?"

"No, I can't fucking call him." Soledad pushed him down in a chair. "You got a gut wound. You left a trail of shit in the hallway."

"I can't feel a goddamn thing." His breathing slowed. "We... we need to move again. What do you think? Florida? Pennsylvania?"

Soledad returned from the bathroom with gauze and scissors. Franco was lost in a chimera of his thoughts. Blood saturated the old chair, dripping onto the floor.

"I have friends there," he said.

"You don't have friends," Soledad said. "Not that I've seen. Just bums and junkies. And stupid criminals. How did you ever let it get to this? *Fuck*."

Franco smiled. There was blood on his teeth. His glance faded out the window down to the streets of Harlem. He stood up and grabbed a paper napkin from the counter. Scribbled something down.

"Last will." He wrote. "And testicle. Ha."

She'd stood holding a roll of gauze when he handed her a poem. The penmanship was so poor she couldn't make it out. Blood had saturated the napkin. He sat back in the chair and faded away.

TWENTY

Cemetery. Soledad stood by the coffin as servicemen lowered it. Dressed all black, even had a wide brim hat that covered her face. All she could do was stare at the ground. Not the casket, not the hole it descended into. Just the dirt.

The sound of a 21-gun salute startled her back to reality. One of her father's cousins was there, but they didn't speak to her. Her mother stood beside her and she anticipated what they were going to say to each other after the service.

Thiago never showed up even though he'd said he would. She was glad he didn't come. He would have been full of excuses and empty apologies.

TWENTY-ONE

She had few options but to go see Thiago. He'd relocated his office closer to Harlem, closer to her. Slowly, she watched his business decline. Desperation set in like black fungus. But work was work as the city consumed them all. Then he blackmailed her.

She opened her apartment door to Leo Kern sitting on the sofa. He wore a nice suit and sunglasses. His hair had recently been re-dyed black. No tie, open collar. He was reading one of her books.

Soledad gave a long pause, neither startled nor phased. Too numb to care. Not afraid because the gun was in her hoodie pocket. He looked unarmed but confident. Dangerous. Kern casually lifted his eyes from the book to her.

"It was a long time coming." He spoke like a dandy, a sociopathic joker. "Sorry I missed the funeral."

She felt her hand sweat around the snubby. He studied all her motions carefully.

"It was... honorable," she said. She closed the door behind her. "You should have been there. Weren't you his drug dealer?"

"Come on, girl." Kern said. "Is that what I fucking look like to you? Perhaps I've misrepresented myself."

"Did he owe you money? There's nothing here. I have nothing. Unless you want that piece of shit TV."

"You have nothing, so it makes you a richer person than I." Kern smiled. So disingenuous, it gave her a chill. "I'm sure there's a proverb somewhere about that. You know it, right? You've read all these books."

He'd been skimming through her copy of *Anti-Oedipus: Capitalism and Schizophrenia*. He closed it and stacked it on top of her other books.

"You're just another one of Thiago's goons," she said. The apartment felt even smaller with whatever sinister plume he'd brought with him. An evil that could fill a warehouse.

"Perhaps, it's the other way around," Kern said.

"You drove Franco around to get fixed and do your dirty work. Kind of makes you a goon. Get out or I'll shoot you."

"Come on. Say it like you mean it. I'm not convinced. Is that a gun you're holding?" Kern raised his hands. "Don't worry, I'll leave soon enough. But hear me out."

"Thiago works for *you*?" She pulled out the .38 snubby and aimed it at him. "Answer my fucking question!"

Kern raised his hands higher. "If you must know, I'm an independent. My bosses vary, city to city, job to job. Thiago and I worked out a business deal. He owed me a debt, so we tooled around and came up with a contract. One thing you learn is that you always need a middleman."

Soledad stepped closer. Pointed directly at him. Pulled the hammer back. Her hand was steady. He countered by staring back.

"You can shoot me," Kern said. "And you'll tell the cops I broke in and attacked you. What happens when they ask you about that gun? You used it to kill Benny and then there'll be questions and you'll have to explain why you did the dirty work for your father."

"It's not like on TV. Cops don't care about details," Soledad said. "You think they have time for that? They're too busy busting heads on people occupying the streets right now. Or shooting black men."

Kern laughed. "They will care if someone sends them ballistic evidence. And photos of the perpetrators. I record and report all things. In fact, I'm recording this conversation right now. It's broadcasting into a little secret box somewhere off premises. Why didn't you ditch it like you're supposed to?"

Soledad lowered the gun. "I keep it for creeps like you. You think I had a choice in any of this?"

"That's the pitiful, *I didn't ask to be born* elective," Kern said. "I've seen everything that's happened. Your father worked for Thiago. I thought their friendship was more profound and tightly fused. Turns out 'Thiggy' will do *anything* to turn a buck. Your father owed him, not matter the work he did."

"Thiggy and I have an agreement to settle that."

"With Franco gone, it leaves one single, unfinished bit of business I had with Thiago and Franco. Don't shoot me. There's still work to be done. Not for Thiago. For me."

"Whatever you had with Franco ended with Franco," Soledad said. "Doesn't extend to me. I'm getting the fuck out of New York as soon as I can. Should have never come to live with my father in the first fucking place."

"Where are you going to?" Kern said. "Do you really have a place to go? There's only one thing I need from you. Then you can go wherever you please. You never have to see Thiago or myself ever again. I'll even get you a plane ticket out of here, so you don't have to ride in some stinking bus. You like that?"

"You don't understand," she said. "I have nothing to give you. I mean, I donated his suits to the rescue mission where we used to live. Whatever he owed I can't pay back."

"It's not money I'm after, dear. There are details I won't divulge right now. But I need you to sit tight in the meantime. Don't leave the city until I say so. For your own protection."

"Franco's death clears the debt. So, fuck you."

"You look tired. I've been desperate, trying to find good help. I didn't really want to use Franco— believe me—but Thiago insisted. I suppose it was a favor he owed him. I've been looking, but it gets harder. Slim pickings. Bottom-of-the-barrel. I find them on street corners, gutters. Violent types but not a lot of brains. You'd be surprised how easy it is to get a transient to do dirty work. Pay them enough and they will kill *anybody*. And then once they're done, I come around and just pop-pop and they're dead. I don't do that part, of course. I pay someone else to clean the cleaner. Clears their conscience and mine. I do dirty work, but I am transparent about my deviancy. Please, don't let me take any more of your time."

He stood up. Hands up, smiling, as he passed her. His gaze and motion towards her were predatory.

"I'll see you in a few days," he said.

He left and she slammed the door shut. Downstairs a car pulled up and he got in it and then it drove away.

TWENTY-TWO

Daylight through the windows of the apartment. Empty spaces but she still felt Franco's presence. She woke up the next day having slept very little, still fully dressed.

She grabbed the gun from the kitchen counter and went into the bedroom to the full-length mirror she'd dug out of a dumpster. She placed the gun at her head, hating her reflection.

TWENTY-THREE

It took a week for Kern to reach out to her. Next thing she was being driven around the city in a big 70's model Chrysler with Maroon interior. Something no longer manufactured. Built like a tank. Sailed like a yacht.

Kern drove.

Soledad wore her jumpsuit and hoodie. Gun in the front pocket. She kept both hands on it.

"Can you believe the rate at which this place is changing?" Kern's tone was almost humorous. "Look at the alarming way the city is...*growing*. The other day I saw a couple— *white people*— jogging up on 115th. They were not afraid. Businesses understand what it takes to clean things up. See all this? *They* own it."

"Who owns it?" Soledad said.

"*They*. Them. *Them*. This will soon be demolished, and they will put a big faceless, soulless box in its place. A trough where white people will come to buy expensive things and consume tasteless foods and wines. Right now, labor is cheap. Materials are cheap. Businesses are champing at the bit to get the ball rolling. They can't wait to see all the white faces that are waiting to move in."

"I know about neo-colonialism."

"You know what the hardest part about this development is? Getting the people who don't want to get up and go, to actually *get up and go*. This Dominican grocer for instance. I'll show you where. We offered money, a new business location, but he just won't leave. Said his grandfather opened the place in the 60's. Imagine that? Holding on so hard and for so long?"

Kern parked on a busy Harlem corner. He pointed to the bodega. The one she frequented.

"I'll drop you off here and wait around the other side of the street," Kern said. "He's going to be closing soon. He's got customers now. Go in. Be friendly. Ask for stuff. After you pay for everything, do it and get out."

Soledad opened the door and stepped onto the sidewalk. The day had a dull chill to it. Kern reached over and grabbed the back of her hoodie and pulled her back in.

"Wait," he said. "Not today. We got a week to do this. Get in. I'll drive you to 5th Ave."

Kern turned on the radio. Something came on from the 1970's. He sang along to it as he drove her back.

TWENTY-FOUR

At the apartment, Soledad sat on the sofa, in her hoodie, head craned out the window, staring at the skyline that seemed fabricated from old paintings.

Curtains fluttered like ragged ghosts. There was a dying plant on the windowsill. The day was overcast but she could see the skyline against the northwest corner of Central Park.

There were times she saw him. The zombified ghost of Franco sitting beside her on the sofa, his skin color going white to green. Blank eyes. Sitting there in his underwear, ghost body bearing the bullet hole that killed him.

TWENTY-FIVE

Several days later. Kern drove her. Different car than last time, a funereal black sedan with tinted windows. Had the feel of a government car. His narration droned, more intense than usual. Manic chatter. Soledad watched the city from the passenger side. She pulled her hood over her head and closed her eyes.

She could barely stand to look at him.

Kern pointed to his left. "Formally Mount Morris, now Marcus Garvey Park. Imagine, whites, who'd once owned black people, forced to include them into their fold. Apologetically renaming avenues and public parks after famous negroes. Frankly, it doesn't matter who lives here tomorrow and tomorrow after. By now you've figured out why I've been sent here. I just don't want you to think that I'm some hatemonger. I'm just a capitalist with a job to do. Even if it's murder. On behalf of the imperialist cause."

Soledad looked at him. "Who are you really working for?"

"*Me*," Kern said. "I work for *me*. Privately contracted but checks arrive from different sources and contacts. I don't ask."

"Your conscience seems at rest." Soledad looked to park on the rocky hill.

"Just working by instinct." Kern's voice droned like public TV narration. "I was once on your side of things. They cry *liberal* and *Marxist*, don't they? But there's no denying that the narrative of both sides is written in blood."

"You're saying there's no winning for the good guys?" she said.

"I'm saying there are no good guys. Only survivors. Murderous lust runs in our bloodstream, including yours and mine. Like a beast of prey, I'm giving in to instinct. If there is such a thing as an objectionable conscience, I want to have the opposite of it. Every time there is a massacre in some African village or Middle Eastern desert town, there I am claiming the real estate on behalf of my bosses."

"You're not participating in any violence. You're paying people to do it for you. You're taking money from higher-ups. That makes you just as much a slave."

"I won't argue that." Kern smiled. "But my hands stay clean. And what is the price for burning a village? What is a man thinking when he slaughters a classroom full of children with a machete? When babies are ripped out of the womb of a crying mother and slaughtered so that the tribe goes extinct?"

"Your conscience pesters you otherwise I wouldn't be here," she said. "Or you wouldn't have had Franco do your dirty work. Essentially, you're a coward, more than you are a slave to your supposed imperialist cause."

Kern laughed. It came out with a sinister roll then turned maniacal. He adjusted his sunglasses. For a moment she could see that one of his eyes was blank. No pupil.

"I'm hip to the sound of a dead body hitting the ground," Kern said. "Bombs dropping from above. I'm tired of the game, but I'm not ashamed of playing. I'm just working the natural order of things. You know all about this. I've seen the literature you subscribe to. I've read your books."

He'd circled around the park a few times. Weekday traffic kept the street busy with buses, cabs, delivery trucks, bicyclists, and pedestrians.

"I no longer have a cause," Soledad said. "I'm for ideals. Some of them work. On paper they *all* work."

"I've watched you," Kern said. "Saw how you slowly degenerated into what your father was. And you are nothing like him. You're a lot like me, actually."

"Don't try to enforce your dominance. I'm just me, man. You haven't got a fucking clue about me."

He chuckled. "You're bordering on being a footnote. You're nothing but a *hoodrat*, as the locals say. But that's why we're having this conversation. I have a feeling you've embraced that desperation, same as Franco. That cutthroat despondency. And you've learned how easy it is to do it. How to pull the trigger. In you I've found a protégé. Why deny it? There will always be a master to the student. Master to servant."

"You're obviously somebody's servant."

Kern stared at her for a long time. Not minding traffic, oblivious to bicyclists, walkers or anything else on the narrow avenue. "When it comes to evolution, how do you think we got so far? *Perversity.* Bloodlust. That's the human currency, the most tangible form of trade is violence."

TWENTY-SIX

Kern parked on a corner diagonal to the bodega. Soledad crossed the avenue, going into the store without a word. There was a belligerent customer at the front counter arguing with the owner. Soledad went to the drink cooler and grabbed a can of tea. The usual misfits weren't hanging out today. The bootleg video rack had been removed.

She went back to the front and the argument had grown truculent. Other customers put down their groceries and left the store.

The belligerent customer shouted and raised his arms, something typically seen in New York every day. Especially Spanish Harlem. Shouting, cursing, throwing out racist rants. The man reached over the counter and grabbed the storeowner. The man Soledad was supposed to kill.

Her gun went off. Sounded like a firecracker. The bodega turned silent but for the humming refrigerators. She shot him again. The store owner nervously backed away, hands raised, covered in the screaming man's blood. The dead man fell over the ice cream cooler and slumped face down on the floor in the blood that gathered.

Soledad aimed the gun at the owner while backing out. She dropped the can of tea and ran, tucking the gun back in her hoodie pocket.

TWENTY-SEVEN

Running. Up the block. All she heard was her boots clocking the sidewalk. Disoriented. The city was the belly of the beast and it was digesting her. She heard screeching tires rounding the corner behind her. She waited for the gunshots. Kern drove up against the curb, parking on the sidewalk.

She slowed to a walk, ignoring him. At the corner, she contemplated. Her feet shifted nervously. She turned around and walked back to his car.

Kern lowered the passenger window and she aimed the gun at him. Kern had his drawn and shot first. The combined blasts were deafening. She got hit but shot back until her gun was empty. Riddled his belly. Hit him where she knew it was impossible to recover from. Or at least put him in a wheelchair shitting into a plastic bag the rest of his life.

The gun fell out of his hand onto the seat beside him. She watched him convulse, watched the blood spread from his stomach up to his chest, and down to his crotch, but didn't stick around to see him die.

She ran down the block, cut west and then ran north. Threw the gun down a storm drain. Blood darkened her hoodie. She pressed her right hand under her left arm, close to her breast where the bullet entered. Blood pulsed through her fingers.

TWENTY-EIGHT

At the apartment Soledad stood naked in front of the long mirror cleaning the wound. Bloody clothes at her feet. With her left arm in the air, she leaned right, splashing rubbing alcohol over it. Blood cascaded down her side to the marble floor.

The bullet had imbedded under her arm, lodging into the fatty deposits at the edge of her latissimus dorsi muscle.

Clipped her wing.

Pulling the flesh open with two fingers she could see in the mirror the dull gray of the slug in the yellow fattiness. Without an anesthetic it didn't hurt so much as stung. Tears welled and her hands shook. She felt nauseous. She'd fixed plenty of Franco's wounds, some worse than this, but it wasn't easy. She used every disinfectant she had and in lieu of stitches crisscrossed duct tape over the hole, then taped gauze over the patchwork.

After putting on fresh clothes she smoked a joint and sat on the floor feeling weak and spent. Later she tossed her bloody clothes in the incinerator. She waited for Franco's ghost, but he didn't visit today. The next day she packed her suitcase and vacated the apartment.

TWENTY-NINE

All the train stations on Malcolm X Blvd. were shut down due to a stabbing. Soledad walked up to the 135th St. station. She was being followed but played it casual. A car slowed down near the curb as she crossed a busy 125th and then turned west. She immediately recognized the car. When it pulled up beside her Thiago opened the back door. Soledad searched the car's interior, expecting to see Kern looking back like some resurrected pallbearer. All she could see was Thiago's frightened eyes looking out at her. The driver was an older looking man wearing a guayabera. Without a word or further consideration, she jumped in, throwing her suitcase on the floorboard. The car sped off west, toward St. Nicholas Ave.

"We gotta get the fuck out of the city." Thiago had removed his suit jacket. His tie hung loosely around his neck, his fat face soaked in sweat. "Things got fucked up, baby girl. *They're* everywhere. Looking for you. Looking for *me*. What the fuck happened? I'm taking my ass to Louisiana. Far away as I can go. Office got ransacked. They sent mens after me! It's you and me now, baby girl."

There was a .45 in his fat hand, laying on its side on his thigh. Pointed at her. He stroked his chin nervously, looking down at the gun and then at her, then at traffic. Tapping his feet, soaking his shirt in sweat.

Soledad reached inside her boot. The *balisong* knife had been gifted to her by Franco's friend and Bruce Lee fanatic, Jose. Franco had shown her where to strap it so it wouldn't fall out if she was running yet keep it within reach. Might even get overlooked during a frisk.

She withdrew it slowly while Thiago ranted. Dropped it in her palm and swung it open, clenching it tightly in her fist. The handle was diecast metal with slot cutouts, the curved blade carbon steel.

The first two or three thrusts into his throat and chest built her momentum. Then her emotions took over. And then the rest was just reckless stabbing. He gasped and gurgled blood. After twitching for several seconds, he died. Drooled and pissed himself.

When the driver realized what was happening, he slammed the brakes in the middle of the avenue. Thiago fell forward, dead against the seat. The driver turned around, wrestling with his seatbelt. He looked from the gore back to her. The bloody knife. She stared back, mouth half-open as if to say something.

He went for a weapon inside his jacket, when she plunged the knife deep into his neck, just below his ear. She'd never seen so much blood come out of a man. On the front seat, windshield, door, windows, her sleeve and hand. She released the knife, leaving it poking out of his neck.

The car rolled slowly into the intersection on a red light. Soledad jumped out and ran, holding her suitcase. A freight truck honked and swerved to miss her as she ran to the sidewalk.

The usual New York City symphony blared followed by screams, hollers and collisions. She walked three blocks until 125th crossed St. Nicolas Ave. If the C was running on time it could take her straight down to Port Authority Bus Terminal.

THIRTY

The elevated train station buzzed with cops. Radios crackled with gibberish traded among the badged and armed. Sirens down in the street. Ambulances and firetrucks on the avenue.

Soledad walked past a cluster of confused police milling around the turnstiles. Patrolmen roamed all the way to the end of the platform. Three men in black suits, wearing sunglasses milled around talking with the cops. New editions of Leo Kern.

The digital schedule showed the train was six minutes away. She squeezed her fingernails into the palms of her hands and realized she had a ring of blood drying on her forefinger and thumb of her right hand.

Bloodstained, the best she could do was wipe down the front of her hoodie and roll up her sleeves.

She found a spot on the platform and waited. To her right, police accosted a young black man who wore a similar hoodie as hers. It was Revolt, from the bodega. They blocked him, harassed and pointed fingers in his face. Revolt was defensive and belligerent.

Soledad looked up at the schedule again. The din of cops drowned out the unintelligible overhead announcements. She closed her eyes and exhaled. Tapped her feet anxiously.

Revolt shouted and argued. Resisted. Five cops surrounded him, along with one of the men in black.

As the train slid into the station Revolt broke into a run, heading toward her. Cops scrambled after him, drawing their guns. The panicked crowd shifted chaotically, shouting and falling over each other in disarray.

The train sat there a good ten seconds without the doors opening.

"*Come on,*" she said impatiently. She wiped sweat from her brow, leaving a streak of blood across her forehead.

Gunshots popped. People panicked and scattered. She turned to see Revolt laying on the platform on his side, bleeding, eyes staring back at her.

The train doors opened, and she shoved her way in. Passengers poured out, stumbling over nervous cops, stepping over the young black man dying from gunshot wounds.

Someone on the platform yelled for her to stop.

"*Stand clear of the closing doors, please.*"

Bing-bong.

The doors shut and the train rolled. On the platform, one of the men in the black suits saw her and pointed. Cops ran alongside the train, waving their guns and shouting. Soledad closed her eyes, placed a hand under her arm where her wound was healing, where it still ached.

Acknowledgement

Thank you to Mark Chilsom for praising the screenplay named *Soledad* which I then turned into this novella you hold in your hands.

Thank you to Shanee because you lived some of this with me.

Thank you DuVay Knox because your suggestions improved it.

Thank you to Tia Ja'nae for her editing and formatting and to Alec Cizak for letting me join the amazing roster at *Uncle B. Publications*.

Thank you to Joni Mitchell, whose masterful album *Mingus* is one of the greatest records ever made and its spirit blesses this book.

Thank you to all the readers who showed love for my debut novel, *Dead Dogs*.

Manny Torres

Biography

Originally from Brooklyn, New York, Manny Torres resides in Atlanta, Georgia. He is also a photographer and painter. He is the author of the road-noir *Dead Dogs,* and its follow-up *Perras Malas,* which will be published in 2022. He's written and directed several documentaries and music videos, including *The Trespasser, Unendangered Species,* and *The Abby Go Go Christmas Special.* For 15 years he was a programmer and co-conspirator on Step Outside: The Strange and Beautiful Music program on WMNF 88.5FM in Florida. He is currently working on a series of crime novels.

Indianapolis, Indiana